When You Die
In
Central Park

When You Die in Central Park

Geneva Grace Kellam

This is a work of fiction. Names, characters, places, and incidents are either the product of the author's imagination or are used fictitiously, and any resemblance to actual persons, living or dead, business establishments, events, or locales is purely coincidental.

Copyright © 2019 by Geneva Grace Kellam

All rights reserved.
Except for use in a review, no part of this book may be reproduced, scanned, or distributed in any printed or electronic form without permission.

For Claree and Leroy and Benjamin

Before

Day or night, noon or shadow, there was always someone running in Central Park. Always someone who was getting up earlier, or putting dinner, or sleep, or sex off a little later, pushing to do another mile, another circuit around the reservoir. Roberta wasn't afraid of running in the park late at night. Running made her feel strong. She looked for her stride. It always came. It would sneak up on her, unnoticed, and she'd be in it before she realized it was there. Sometimes it came right outside her front door. Sometimes she ran jerky the entire four miles, stiff legged and wrong the whole way out and back again, and only the last full-out sprint before she stopped would feel right. Tonight around ninety-sixth street she had it, a solid pace, elastic legs, a ride on the rhythm. Taking a run had been the right thing to do. Something to make up for the crummy day that she'd thought would be picture perfect.

Sitting at the Bontemps luncheon this afternoon, she'd fully expected to win for outstanding new black literature. Roberta knew she'd deserved it last year, too, and would have gotten it except one of the other short-listed writers had died of AIDS during the judging. Posthumous beats present – even writing contests have unwritten rules. But this year? This year the book she'd finished was better. More mature, more well resolved, wittier. All three of the major reviews said so. (One had used that rankling "promising," but Robbie tried not to dwell on it.)

The Bontemps came with money. Not life-changing money. Ten thousand dollars. Enough to feed some fantasies. Enough for a new suit and a pocketbook that would impress people in a way Roberta's knapsack most certainly did not. At her table Roberta had been so busy imagining herself mulling through Saks she barely tasted the quiche the waiter brought, or the wine. With the salad came a daydream of opening an account at Bendel's. Chewing the fish she chose fabric for Roman shades for the living room. How many years had it been since she could enjoy spending? She couldn't remember. As the dessert dishes disappeared Roberta was picturing her daughter on a beach meeting the Caribbean, now that she was walking. The room had stilled in anticipation as time came to announce the winner. The pleasant tingle of silver on crystal lingered in the air. Roberta was already halfway standing when the lady at the podium said:

"Cynthia Cox."

Cynthia Cox? Cynthia Cox! Cynthia Cox had barely enough talent to write a check. Already out of her seat and too embarrassed to sit back down, Roberta continued the excruciating rise to her feet and clapped, and slowly the room joined her.

No way could Roberta not have joined Cynthia for a drink after. It would have made the ovation look insincere. Nor could Roberta have refused to go to Cafe La Fortuna for opera and dessert. Not with Cynthia exclaiming how Robbie had to come. Could she have said no to tumbling into the cab downtown? Robbie never allowed herself a cab. If she didn't want to stomach the subway, she took the bus. Or walked. But today, with all the other black writers, it would have looked cheap. And then the champagne at Chambers. Could she have bowed out then? Not with the group dwindling so small and Cynthia growing sentimental, which made her whining manner of speaking all the more pronounced. Even Cynthia's jokes sounded like complaints. And of course, she was being phonily modest. “I’m touched and honored. So many other books were so good this year.”

“So many other books were better. Like mine,” Robbie said. But not aloud. Cynthia paid nothing. Robbie enjoyed nothing. Had she really eaten an entire slice of cheesecake? Just because she was eating the cost didn’t mean she had to consume the calories, too. Judgment was a fatality of alcohol. She was half drunk when she called and told John not to wait up and to kiss the baby for her. All the way drunk when she got home. Roberta hated how her fellow passengers on the elevator, a friendly old couple who lived on ten, were hugging the wall to increase the space between her and them. Heretofore they’d probably thought of her as “that nice colored girl upstairs.” Not any more. Now they’d talk about how she couldn’t hold her liquor and how black people didn’t know how to do things in moderation. How embarrassing.

She’d asked the elevator operator to let her off on eight; she’d walk the rest of the way.

“You sure?” Danny said.

Most days she walked up from the lobby. Walking from eight would be no problem. Sober, anyway. “Sure.”

Danny’d slid the cage door open; Roberta could still feel him and the old couple watching as she stepped into the hallway and pushed through the fire door to the back stairs. She made sure it didn’t slam.

She heard John snoring as soon as she opened the apartment door. John snored like he was pretending to be asleep. The one rebel thing she’d done in her life was marry an actor. He got to be the artiste in the family. In the mornings he got to kiss Roberta goodbye in his robe and underwear, his mug of fresh-brewed coffee in his hand while she went off to an office. So what that he was crazy about her? He wasn't the one cramming his writing into nights and weekends. She was the one who looked like a fool while he worked out, took classes, went on the occasional audition. They dreamed of his big break, the movie role that would catapult him to millions, of her best-seller that would buy them a house in the country, with maybe a pool, and a separate outbuilding she could work in. In the meantime, they lived in a one-bedroom in a transitional neighborhood. In the meantime, their baby daughter slept in an alcove by the kitchen in an alcove that used to be the pantry.

From birth, Paloma was blessed with her father's elegant limbs and so far, his heavy blond curls. Robbie was amazed that this child had come out of her nappy self with so little kink. Paloma had the sweet baby smell. And the poopy smell. Paloma didn't seem to be bothered by it at all, but Roberta thought her little heinie would be more comfortable in a fresh diaper. Funny how wine made some things so urgent and others negligible. Roberta moved quietly in the moonlight that turned Paloma's hair silver, lifted the diaper hamper lid and let it down with care, tucked the sheet, all done. All quiet, except John's snores.

Even with his mouth open and his briefs sagging, John was handsome. Robbie stood still in the bedroom entrance and looked at him. She smelled his smell, unique to him, the smell his apartment had before she moved in. If he had awakened and said, "Don't go out now. What're you, crazy?" Roberta would have argued with him and not gone. With the exaggerated care of the inebriated, she pulled her running clothes from this morning out of the dirty clothes basket they'd bought for pennies in Marrakesh; opening the drawers for clean would have made too much noise.

That midnight was bright with a high, orange moon, and warm, about seventy-five degrees. She'd run crosstown out of sync. At West End, Broadway, Amsterdam, Columbus, Manhattan, Central Park West, at every avenue, the lights were red against her. And then she was in the park.

Taking her punishment. For drinking too much and eating too much, for not being thin enough, or popular enough, or productive enough, or tall enough or enough in all the other areas where she fell short. But she was running. She was regaining her virtue.

She loved this park. The East Side, staid, old, envied, arrogant, and the West Side, with its revolutionaries and upstart successes, the two converged in Central Park and stopped their competition in favor of sunbathing and kite flying and reading on an old blanket. She loved the statues of writers, angels, falconers, politicians and pets, the promenades, the fountains, the woods and lakes. She liked the ponds and bridle paths. She felt better. The evening hadn't been so bad. She'd met some new people. She'd taken some pictures with the judges and Cynthia. Maybe she'd be mentioned in a caption. It was something. At least she could stop beating herself up for her arrogance in not networking – she'd made time today for sure. She still thought it shouldn't make any difference who you went to B. Smith's with; writing didn't get any better because you were friends with the judges. Or any worse if you weren't.

Roberta felt good. Good to be in the warm night. Good to be running, to enjoy the heat at the bottom of her soles. She hummed down the hill at Eighty-third Street. A taxi came over the hill behind her, hit her and sent her flying. She thudded on the asphalt twenty feet away.

Staring at the broken woman, the poor taxi driver lost most of his English. He lost some time crying over her small body, but he was able to radio his dispatcher who hastened an ambulance right away. The ambulance drivers didn't have far to come, and they came, lights flashing, quickly. They got to the woman under target time. They saw she had sturdy legs, a tight little waist, and modest bulges in her upper arms. She looked strong. The ambulance personnel felt they could save her.

At the hospital, the emergency staff tried to pump breath into her body and to stimulate her heart with electricity. They worked on her for forty-five minutes. By then she was resting on the back side of the Maine Monument between War and History, under the arms of Justice.

Death

The early noises of rush hour niggled at the edge of her sleep and her sleep absorbed them. But shoe leather scraping sidewalk grew from whisper to hiss to steady crunch and the subway's rolling rumble grew constant and was joined by car horns and brakes and screeching tires. There's no hitting the snooze button on midtown in the morning. Roberta opened her eyes and pulled herself up to look over the edge of the seashell chariot at the southwest edge of Central Park. It seemed to her that she was cold, and nestled against the statue she reflected that she didn't like cold and that the feeling she had was pleasant. So it wasn't cold; more like a low-grade chill, like walking into an air-conditioned store from a hot street. She felt it especially in her fingertips. She wondered if that was her fingernails still growing. They say your nails grow for weeks after you're dead. Even though the sun rose and the air warmed, the vague tingling continued. When the sun was above the buildings in the east and the crowd heading to work waned, she climbed down, over the stone men, past the live pigeons and walked uptown in the park.

She went by the hill where the cab struck her. An out-of-body experience that. Shooting up and forward and thud on the pavement. No sign that she had died there. No dark spot, nothing that looked like blood, unless that oil spot wasn't oil? She wondered if she'd bled. She was fine now. Amazing how well she felt, really. She'd been hit on the back on the right she figured; yet her back felt fine on both sides. She felt light, limber. Her shorts were looser around her waist. Dipping below her navel, definitely. Nice. She shrugged her shoulders and shook her arms and legs loosely the way she'd seen Olympic athletes do on TV. She bet if she took a running start, reached her elbows up beside her ears, bent her knees and pushed off, she could fly. She thought about trying, and thought it would look silly. It would. Still, she felt better than she'd ever felt in her life.

At the 72nd Street entrance on Central Park West there are benches where mornings, the mothers chat with each other and drink their second coffees while their children nap in strollers. In the afternoon the old people come out to complain while they catch some vitamin D. Out-of-workers and freelancers sit there too, when they want to get outside but haven't the money to spend in the restaurants and stores. Before the road curves down in into the park drive, away from the constant crowd at the Imagine medallion, Bruce and Ed tanned their chests. Bruce balanced his head against the top edge of the backrest, thrusting his feet far onto the sidewalk. In flattened flip flops they were beautifully articulated feet, carefully turned out, one set of toes facing the American Museum of Natural History, the other pointing toward the Metropolitan Museum of Art. Bruce didn't have a perfect one hundred eighty degrees turnout; he'd come late to dance at seventeen. Heels together, knee backs together, thighs pressed hamstring to hamstring into a solid, symmetrical mass. He loved how it looked from his vantage point, wished he could do it standing up.

Bruce and Ed. Roberta had always liked them. She leaned over Ed's shoulder to look at the paper. He held it down in his lap so as not to block the sun. Roberta's body didn't make a shadow. Her obit lay open.

"What time tomorrow is the funeral?" Bruce asked.

Her funeral. She wondered what she was going to wear. She had a beautiful suede mock turtleneck that hadn't fit her since before the baby that she felt would look good on her now. Her mother'd probably pick out some fashion-free babyish bull with puffed sleeves. She made a quick mental run-through of her closet. Good. No puffed sleeves or shirtwaists, another style her mother liked on her. John would be powerless against her mother; more accurately, he wouldn't care.

"Ten o'clock." Ed rustled the newspaper. It hit Roberta in the face. No "Sorry," no "Oh, excuse me." It was as if Roberta weren't there. But look how much ink the *Times* had given her! They'd included her Off-Off Broadway one-act, the two novels, even her advertising awards; details about one's life only employers know. It always helps to keep your resume current. A picture, too. From the Bontemps.

"With Cynthia Cox." Bruce said. "Robbie would die." His laugh stuck in his throat.

"I've got to get my black suit pressed," Ed announced. He stood.

Bruce kept his eyes shut against the sun as he turned his face toward Ed. "You'll never make it. It won't be ready until after the funeral's over. You're always leaving things to the last minute."

"Oh, loosen up. People like spontaneity. You could use more." Ed said.

Roberta felt a pang of guilt. Bruce was the nicer person, but she had always had more fun with Ed. He made her feel like the most expensive treat in the shoppe. He knew all the best gossip and the cheapest sample sales. He got royal treatment at restaurants. Nobody denied him anything, thanks to his undeniable looks, which would be all gone by the time he was thirty-five. But he had just turned thirty-one and left broken hearts in his wake.

"Get a new suit," Bruce said, rising. "You need it. I'll buy it for you." Ed sat down. He stood up. He leaned over Bruce and rested his lips against his lover's forehead. "Come with me now," he said.

"Who's that?" Someone said into Roberta's ear and she jumped clear across the bench. A man she hadn't heard coming, or felt coming, medium tall, with thick hair and plenty of shoulders for it to rest on, stood next to where she used to be standing. He was wearing a loincloth and he raised his hand in a "How" gesture, like Hollywood Indians in 50's westerns. He came in peace.

Roberta caught her breath, and assessed. In truth, the only thing scary about the guy was his approach. He was pretty. A dark lock curled damply on his smooth forehead. The man was made to have his picture taken. Roberta nearly laughed aloud, amusement and nerves. "Love your outfit," she said. What could he do to her, after all? Kill her?

"What do you call the big one?"

"Ed."

"I imagine that's you they're reading about? I was a news item, too, so I heard. 'Murder in Ramble.' I was the tail end of a tiny trend." He nodded toward the gay couple. "I love it." He hugged himself. "These boys are so free to be. Not like when I was here. I was killed very near here for doing very near the same thing. Times change.

"I'm Ivan." Pronounced Yvonne. He offered his hand.

"Roberta Williams. Robbie." She didn't like the feel of him. Cool and raw, just barely too cool to be clammy. Like thrusting one's hand into dirty mop water with a glove with a hole in it. He didn't feel alive. Nor did he feel dead, not entirely. What did dead feel like? Dry, probably. Like fallen leaves.

"I feel cold to you?" he said. "You feel warm to me. Close to live." Bruce and Ed were walking away. Robbie made to pull her hand, but Ivan held it. "You can't leave. Let me tell you a few things." He pulled her toward the lake.

"I'm dead. I know already."

"No shit, Sherlock."

"Is this Purgatory? Because I'm not Catholic."

"This is Central Park."

"Does that mean that the East Side is Heaven?"

"Good one." He smiled, licked the tip of his forefinger and drew a short vertical in the air. "It means you liked it here. People who loved the park and die in the park get to, as psychologists call it, work out their issues in the park."

"I hope that means that people who litter in the park and die in the park go straight to Hell," she said. To herself.

"You're not alone," he continued. He guided her east, past the bowling green. "On the other hand, we're a pretty loose community. I'd imagine you'll like most of us; we pretty much fit into a narrow demographic band. Who else dies in the park but the young and the foolish? Which were you?"

"I was always the most cautious of people. I slept with the windows locked and the gates locked over my windows."

"And you weren't out running at midnight." Touché. "I used to see you running," he said. "I admired your determination."

If there was anything about herself Robbie admired, it was her determination. Steady daily work had been her magic wand. It had turned lumpy legs into sleek ones, her obsession with work into dedication. She hadn't been one of the young overnight people who parleyed youth into genius. She'd been a plodder. Working with her thoughts was craft, not talent, unless talent had to do with determination, exercise, practice making perfect. Her brightest insights had come not in a flash, but a nugget at a time, after filtering through shovelfuls of shit.

Where was this place? Where were all the people? The traffic noise? Even the sun disappeared moment to moment. Had they passed that bend in the pond before? Roberta wasn't sure. She thought she knew the park, but this was foreign landscape, curvy and condensed.

"You may have noticed already that your clothing is hanging on you. Life keeps weight on you. You've already lost five to seven pounds." Robbie was fascinated. "Within twenty-four hours after you're buried, your temperature will drop twenty degrees. It can be nauseating, but there are ways to make that time more pleasant.

"After you're buried you won't walk the same any more. As soon as they throw dirt over you, gravity repels you. You stop touching the ground. Usually that happens in a day, maybe a week. I was buried right away. Not well, but they tried. The poor bastards had only what they had on hand to dig with. Impromptu. I was killed right there. He pointed north and his deltoids rose.

"What a feast the Ramble used to be. There was mystery - the glimpses of sweating faces in the short flare of a match light. All cool people smoked then, not like now. I think what I miss most is smoking.

"Later on, you'll lose blood. Also, you won't be able to read anymore, once you're buried. You can see but the letters and numbers will become unintelligible. I know what some signs say, but only from memory. It's all Greek to me, otherwise. Metaphorically speaking. If you could read Greek, you still wouldn't be able to tell."

"I have to read. I'm a writer."

"That's done."

Roberta took off uptown. All her life writing had been her shield. Writing pushed her sail open and powered her through. In a city where there was a constant crop of fresh immigrants drunk on the experience of having black people to look down on, she had survived as a black woman behind the clear protection of accepting their ignorant behavior as raw material and turning it into easily shared packages of language. She could capture a complete experience on the corner of an envelope. No out-of-work mother could stretch a dollar further than Robbie could stretch a word. That couldn't be over.

Robbie ran. She had things to do. A baby to take care of. To bathe and hold and feed and sing to and make up stories for and walk around the living room in the middle of the night. She had to follow up on whether *People* had sent her money yet; if *Women in Business* was buying her pitch. She had a home that wasn't here in the woods. Would her grandparents be there? Poor Mommy and Daddy. Robbie stopped thinking and concentrated on moving her feet. She ran against the traffic coming down the park drive. If she built up enough speed, she could force her way out of the park, out of death. Why not? Stranger things had happened, she was sure. After all, she hadn't seen any warm, white light. Weren't dying people supposed to see a warm, white light, and then a man in a tunnel of brightness beckoning to them? She'd seen none of that. Not a thing. From striking the blacktop to waking up in the Maine

Monument, all was blank. She ran faster. Coming up the Winter Drive she envisioned her feet moving in circles, the pavement just one point on a rapid revolution. She pumped down the hill at 99th Street, arms knifing, knees lifting, head nodding, her breath pouring out and gushing in. She soared out of the park through the entrance at 103rd Street.

She bounced back in.

Incredulous, she made a furious leap. A pressure snapped her back like Costello in *The Time of Their Lives*. It was invisible and impenetrable, as if she and the space outside the park were two magnet ends with like poles repelling each other. She couldn't leave.

Robbie hoisted herself onto the top of the stone wall and sat with her regrets. That she'd never lived in Italy. Back in her files she had a folder stuffed with clippings about Salerno, the small hotels of Rome, Venice in winter. Why hadn't she flown over? Why hadn't she learned to sing? To make fireworks? Why hadn't she gone to the beach more often? An hour and a half to Jones Beach by train and bus. God! She missed the beach.

All her plans. The house searches in Wilmington, North Carolina; between Kingston and Port Antonio; the apartment swap in Turin; even when they'd seemed possible, like that shot at a summer in Montreal, she'd never pulled the trigger. What if they'd laugh at her French? What if the rumors of corrupt police were true? What if she and John couldn't keep up the payments? She'd tossed her dreams like a net over a sea of lovely possibilities and yanked them back empty before they'd hit the water. Why had she been so quick to see the litter, smell the piss? Now it all seemed so warm and comforting. Life, all of it, seemed so damn cool.

So warm. Like yellow sticks of margarine coming to room temperature on a kitchen table, years ago, laid out by her mother to make a cake. Her mother made great cakes. Roberta wept for those cakes and her mother and her father. Her husband. He was going to have a tough time. He couldn't take care of himself, how was he going to take care of Paloma? He'd probably have to give up acting. The very sacrifice she'd been egging him to make. She could see now that would be a loss. He was a good actor.

Her daughter. Her daughter. Her pure giggle. Her gummy grin. Her fat little arms and fingers with their razor nails. The deep red spot between her eyebrows when she cried. The joyful peace that settled in Robbie's body when Paloma slept on Robbie's chest.

There are good things about sudden death for the one who dies. No lingering illness, no long-term pain, no knowledge that the people who love you are suffering with you, whispering behind doors about you and wearing false, courageous smiles to your face for your protection. Fine things to be missed. Robbie would have borne the feeble-mindedness, the flabbiness, the incontinence, to have been able to complete things, to protect the future as much as she could. She'd made no provision to get Paloma through college. Her savings wouldn't cover the apartment maintenance for more than a year or so. So her daughter, her spendthrift husband, her perfect little novel still locked in her mind, save for a few precious pages deep in a computer file mixed with copy for hair care products – when these things slipped under the door of her mind Robbie shoved them back out through the gap they came in through, then stuffed it and covered it up.

A gang of boys came down the hill above the pond at 103rd Street. They were carrying tin cans and other bits of metallic trash. From far away, they looked handsome; dark and slim and loose limbed, but as they came nearer, chanting and snarling, Robbie could see their malformations, the bent digits, the gaps between the teeth. The bands of beggars in Morocco had been the same when she and John had gone there before they married. But then she remembered not to think of John, and when the thought knocked again she pretended she wasn't in. The group stopped close upon her.

"You new here?" the biggest one said. His bottom-heavy face was ugly the way teenage boys are sometimes ugly, unfulfilled, with undecided hair sprouting dirtily above his upper lip.

The rest of his group, five ragged boys, enclosed her in a half circle. "What can they do to me now?" she thought. She said:

"I've lived here all my life."

"That was then," the boy said. "You're new. Fresh meat." He leered. His friends laughed low, rumbling chuckles. The boy's eyes leeched onto hers. All her life she'd been afraid of policemen, dark streets, of being caught when she smoked her little reefer. She had been a physical coward, terrorized by the possibility of violence. Fear had pressed her into a safe life. But it hadn't made her stupid. Scared or no, she still knew the importance of image. So although at the moment Robbie was sniveling and quivery, she knew better than to show it. She held her eye on the ugly boy's eye.

"You've got a lot to learn," the ugly boy said. Mutant misfit with epidermis flaking off his pocky face. "Maybe I'll teach you. Huh."

"Get away from her." It was Ivan, shooing the boys away like so many housecats. With a jerk of their leader's head, they clanged back the way they'd come.

"You've met our Fauves. Wild ones."

"What's up with them?"

"They made themselves known to livings. If you interfere with life, you lose your chance to go on to Heaven. And to add insult to injury, interfere with a living once, you can't do it again. Those boys have given up their future for stupid things like holding onto a living's arm on Hallowe'en. Shaking tree limbs when there is no wind. Keep an eye on them."

"They didn't seem dangerous to me." She didn't know why she said it. Maybe if she acted tough, like she wasn't scared, like it was a joke, and she could take a joke, it wouldn't happen again.

Ivan tossed his hair. "Just because they're just boys doesn't mean they can't cut you or maim you. Did I tell you we don't heal?"

"Why did I have to die here?" she said.

"We all died here," Ivan said.

"I was still young." Robbie said. "Relatively."

"So was I, thank God. Getting stuck here after you lost your looks would be disaster.

"I died in that last great era of white boy cool. Chet Baker, James Dean and Ed 'Cookie' Burns, from 77 Sunset Strip. They don't make 'em like us anymore." Ivan floated across the patchy grass. "I'm sorry about earlier. I laid out the rules kind of rough. But you can take it, right?" He punched her on her arm, harder than just friendly. She held on to her tough girl pose.

"There's somebody I've got to introduce you to. Let's go." Robbie didn't see where she had a lot of options. She climbed down from the wall, whisked the grit off the seat of her shorts and the back of her legs and followed Ivan.

"So this is the girl?" The Duchess tilted her head back and tried to look down her nose at Robbie. Holding straight to her full stiff height, The Duchess was not quite an inch short of the bottom side of five feet. She had knobby elbows and bony knees that poked out from her long thighs. Except for filthy opera-length gloves, she had no clothes on. She'd lost them all, finally, to more than one hundred years' of weather, but she'd held on to her pride and refused to wear cast-offs. She'd also held onto her jewels, which decorated most of her high, proud chest and many of the dainty, grimy fingers of her gloves. Emeralds were her favorites, and they spread around her elegant neck in three tiers. Double rows of diamonds connected the marquis cut emeralds that matched The Duchess' eyes. A nearly obscene glistening of gems encircled her right ankle.

"She's not that incredible," The Duchess assessed. "One Negress I had was much more beautiful. Of course, she was three-quarters white. Hardly a trace of Black blood in her face. But her temper! The blackest temper I ever saw. I can't tell you how often I thought, 'My God! That woman is going to strike me!'" Her gloved hand pressed against her narrow chest, she turned to Ivan. "But she is certainly pretty. Nearly worth a gem all by herself."

"Remember you said that," Ivan said.

"Nearly," she repeated, raising one eyebrow. "Hmmm?" She addressed Robbie. "Well, I am delighted to meet you." With gentle pushes from her thumb, The Duchess shoved a cracked and wrinkled glove down her skinny forearm to her bony wrist where it hung, a crusty puddle, while she drew off each ring in what seemed to be a ritual, for she murmured little names and remembrances over each removal. After receiving a kiss, each ring was dropped into the cupped palm of a silent, watching Black adolescent girl a pace behind The Duchess.

"People say I have names for my jewels. How foolish. It isn't true. They are only extremely costly rocks. But every time I take one off, I remember the sweet history of how it came to me." A large ruby fell into the waiting palms. A birthday present? A gift from an uncle? A lover? Robbie had one diamond, a gift from her parents when she married. John hadn't provided a diamond and Robbie's mother thought it was important she have one. Robbie didn't wear her rings running. Her fingers swelled, and what if she were mugged? Compared to The Duchess' Robbie's fingers looked incomplete. The Duchess tugged at her gloved fingertips, each in a row, coaxing the grayed fabric over each knuckle; thumb, forefinger, middle finger, ring finger, pinky, back to the middle finger of the glove, shake, shake, shake, and a slight tug until the whole glove slipped like a loose skin and she grasped the glove by its fingertips.

"On the day I was shot in a duel over me, I had, in my possession, twelve dozen pair of gloves. I have many more pair. Hidden. Not even Seneca knows where." Robbie was willing to be bet that Seneca, the child-in-waiting, knew. That she could take The Duchess' gloves any time she wanted. Her dark eyes were steady, resting heavy where they watched, then stalking on to gather up more. This was a girl who liked knowledge. Seneca was a student, not a businesswoman, and academia's loss.

The Duchess drew off the first glove. The beauty of her right hand made its match, her left, a miracle. The nails, small and oval, were a creamy color, buffed to a quiet polish. Robbie took the offered hand unaware what a rare thing she was touching. She felt the same loose wetness she felt in Ivan's mushy grasp. She forced herself not to pull away so as not to offend. Robbie wasn't sure whether she was proud of herself for being so socially skillful, or resentful that The Duchess didn't recognize the favor.

"People laugh at me behind my back, I know they do," The Duchess confided, "but no one has hands like mine." She turned them before her admiring eyes as if she were examining for cut, clarity and color.

"Come with me. I'll tell you about my jewels."

"I've heard it all before," Ivan said. "Enjoy." He left. The Duchess drew her gloves back on and claimed her rings from the child.

The whole park wore an air of privacy. Few cars, great silence, dim sky, the changes in light so subtle under the clouds. From Alice's statue up to The Meer the foggy air was a pale shimmering. The wind was steady, but gentle. If you were running around the big loop that early evening, you may have seen three thin outlines walking, drizzle sliding against them, lying against them briefly before slicing through. Ghost figures in the rain. That was Robbie and The Duchess, and Seneca behind.

"Once," The Duchess chirped, "of an afternoon, this park was filled with carriages. Such fun we had. Racing along the drive. Every Sunday afternoon between dinner and supper, we ladies would settle into our families' carriages. The best were made by Mr. Brewster and company. My family had two of Mr. Brewster's famous carriages.

"My father was a very wealthy man. He made a great fortune in the South during the War Between the States and settled on the West Side of Manhattan." The Duchess glinded at an uneven pace. Wraiths that had no rhythm before death are often like that. She moved almost as up and down and start and stop as Robbie walking.

"He was self-made, as was usual in those days for a second son. He enjoyed some small fame, or perhaps infamy. I enjoyed some small renown for my jewels. Mr. Cruickshank himself engraved my picture wearing some of my jewels.

"My father wanted to send me on a trip abroad. Dingy London, glittering Paris, decadent Rome, tidy Geneva, perhaps even Cairo. I convinced him to buy me jewels instead. After all, my husband, when I married, could show me Europe; I had no interest in capturing a title. So many wealthy American girls were taken across the pond and paraded through old castles with too little heat and too many bills unpaid. I wasn't eager for old Europeans with musty pasts. I liked moneyed American boys with futures.

"My father was so taken with his daughter's good sense, he gave me these emeralds," she stopped to finger the green stones, large as postage stamps, her dirty glove tips fondling the biggest, which sat in the hollow of her neck. "I was always very beautiful. Whenever I was feeling unhappy, I could look in the mirror and cheer myself." She sighed.

The Duchess, although tiny, was elegantly proportioned. Long limbs, pale, clear skin, bright red hair. Her eyes were wide, her lips round and pink. But it wasn't a matter of coloring that made her lovely. It was the skull underneath the skin that was most remarkable. Even with the plumpness and gloss life all gone, she was still striking.

"Men were more plentiful than jewels. You may think me a terrible woman, but I knew that dear Roger and my darling Thomas were dueling over me on the morning of 23 March. I came to watch. Wicked of me, I know. I was standing not too far from my carriage when their guns went off. One of the bullets struck me. A tragic accident."

Later, Ivan laughed about that. "She always claims it was an accident. But you've met her. One of those boys shot her. Maybe both. If we didn't lose the wounds that took us out she'd be carrying two bullet wounds to the chest."

"How long has she been here?"

"The park wasn't even finished. A hundred years? A hundred fifty?"

"But people usually go to Heaven much faster than that, right?"

Ivan smiled gently, a Buddha smile. "She has been here longer than anyone else." He reached for Robbie, who withdrew. "You may not believe me now, but being here isn't so bad," Ivan said. "Want to go to a party?" Night was coming. Trees were turning to shadows. Bushes were taking monster shapes.

"I hope it lasts 'till it's light outside."

It was so hard keeping up, Robbie wondered if Ivan really wanted her to come along. She skip-hopped to match his speed, then admitted to a steady jog, but the distance between her and Ivan lengthened, his long, bright form skating across the landscape as if pulled by invisible string, her shorter form jouncing after. They went one, then the other, between the wire backstops of the ball fields, heading due downtown past the tennis courts and the Belvedere Castle with its pond that looked larger in the dark, before Ivan stopped. He waited, pearly in the moonlight, his hair a halo.

"I forgot how slow you new ones are. You're our first in ages. It's odd. We'll get one or even two in a season, and then no one for years and years. Remind me to slow down if I'm going too fast. I'm sorry." Soon he was way ahead again, a receding dot in Robbie's sight. How bad did she want to go to this party? Not at all. She wasn't good at rooms of new people. But then again, she was worse at being outside in the dark alone. She caught up with Ivan at The Bandshell.

"Once upon a time," Ivan said, "there were sheep grazing here." He pointed southwest toward the Sheep Meadow. "Oh, yes. And cows, too. You know The Dairy, don't you? They had cows in The Dairy for milk for the city's poor children. The Duchess knows all about it. We could ask her about it tonight if she came to these things. Which she doesn't. They're embarrassing for her."

"Why?"

"There's a chance, she thinks, that someone will ask her when she's having her party. Who would do that? Why? Shows you how dismal the workings of her mind that she thinks anyone would be that mean. It'll happen for her when she's ready, just like everybody else." He rolled his eyes. Ivan stopped beneath a tree. "We're here."

Robbie looked all around. The Indian Hunter statue behind her nearly breathed in the moonlight. The Mall rolled out before her. It was lush and serene, the leaves thick and shiny overhead, the promenade ending in a vaulted ceiling of stars below which the skyline glowed. Ivan dropped his head back and pointed his chin toward the sky. He drew his lips back over his teeth and forced a noise up from his neck. A bark! In response, a rope ladder dropped from above between them.

"I'll teach you how to do that," Ivan said. "I'm going to teach you self-defense, too. You're way too scaredy."

Who was this guy? What kind of being was he to move and vocalize like an animal? How much culture and how much wild was mixed in his makeup, Robbie wondered. "Up you go," Ivan said. "Want a boost?"

Up Robbie climbed. Below her, Ivan held the ladder stable until she reached leaf cover. They brushed her face, slid along her shoulders, along her arms as the ladder swayed with every step and grasp. Leaves slipped along her thighs and slapped her calves. She did not look down.

"Almost there," she heard Ivan say. It was hard to see with plant in her face, stems trying to poke her eyes. The ladder ended at a vision more wondrous than Jack's giant.

She stepped onto a platform with a rope around the perimeter within a canopy of maple leaves, lush green and white in the moonlight. About two dozen dancing people crowded the floor, freestyling on their own, or cha-cha-ing in a hands-to-the-hips-in-front-of-you line snaking its patternless way about the room. In the center a woman in a floor-length red dress with most of its beads belted out, "Mi corazon, mi alma, mi amor." Her accompaniment, a combo forcing waves of rhythm from sticks, wore nothing but smiles. There were skirts of fresh maple leaves, one full tails, a bicycle outfit and another pair of running shorts, but most people were in tatters amounting to nearly nothing. Even so, the rags were artfully arranged, put together to enhance. A woman with no bra bunched her bit of fabric into a flower for her waist.

"This is more exclusive than Studio 54," Ivan said into Robbie's ear. The people were certainly beautiful. It wasn't just that they were dancing that made them look like dancers. Every one of them could have been the model for a health club. They were ripped, cut, fatless. Robbie felt like a pudge bucket. Across the room a boy, maybe sixteen, laughed constantly. Revelers approached him, kisses fluttered around him, gifts passed into his hands.

"That's Raul. It's his party." Ivan said.

"It's his birthday?"

"We don't have birthdays. Small favors, right? We don't have deathdays, either." Ivan grinned. "They're giving Raul gifts to deliver to their relatives and friends in Heaven. It's all nonsense of course. Heaven's got to be packed. The possibility of running into anyone you know or anyone you know knows has got to be astronomical."

"He's going to Heaven?"

"Everyone does, eventually." The subject bored him. "You get dreams. From what I hear they're different for everybody, adjusted to personal iconography. Raul saw Madonnas. One old geezer dreamt of Mother Russia. He knew he was going soon when he saw himself bathing in a sea of wodka." In the music's ebb, Ivan eased Robbie a few feet forward. The music caught half a breath and began again. "You get three dreams. The first is a promise; no one who gets the first dream fails to get the second and third. After your last one, you give a non-voyage party for the ones who aren't going yet. This is Raul's non-voyage."

Robbie wished she hadn't come. The energy was high, but it didn't lift her. In all the dancing and laughing, she felt unconnected. She identified what was missing. Rhythm. She heard it, but she didn't feel it. No pulse came though the floor, rumbling into her nerve endings. The tumblers fell into place. No one's feet but hers were touching the platform. Everyone else danced on air about three inches above the floor. Robbie didn't just feel fat, but short, too.

She didn't catch anyone at it, but she knew eyes were on her. On her brown skin. Her round thighs, her overripe rear, her overtight calves, her short dreadlocks that stood up like Buckwheat's hair. She felt eyes staring directly, sliding sidelong in their sockets from under half-lowered lids. She felt them sucking at every flaw, lingering hotly over every embarrassing bump. She felt whispers, too, hissing around her ears with the cheeky insistence of flies. She felt sodden among these people. She was as self-conscious as a high schooler alone at the same party as her ex and his new girlfriend.

"Come on," Ivan said. He touched her arm, then pointed a long, dirty hand toward a rough staircase. "Let's go on upstairs."

It was a short climb between tree branches to the top level. Ivan crossed the empty floor to a group of four men. The tallest man rested his elbow on the shortest man's shoulder.

"Hi, Yvonne," the short one said. He was missing a front tooth; on his face it looked adventurous.

"Hiya, lover," the tall one said. "Who's new?"

Introductions. Everest was the tall one. Bart, the short one, and two dark-haired men, one in a blue serge three-piece suit, were Simon and Morrison.

"I never knew all this was here," Robbie said.

"Ole Bob Redman built his tree houses well," Everest allowed. His talk was slow. Robbie had heard voices like his in North Carolina. Sexy men who could do anything they set their minds to. Fix truck engines. Hunt possum in the dark. Make babies. Beyond the leaves brisk clouds marched across the moon.

Bart talked fast. "The Parks Department found a few and tore them apart. But there are still a few the Parks Department doesn't know about. . ."

"Or chooses to ignore." Everest said.

Bart continued. "Redman build them all over. He hauled up the planks one at a time under cover of darkness using ropes and pulleys. He put them all together without driving a single nail into a single tree. He named them after stars. His last one was Epsilon Eridani. It wasn't far from here. The park rangers found him in it. They destroyed the tree house. But the Conservancy gave him a job as a tree climber and pruner." Bart took a breath. "Do you like that story? It's true."

Robbie nodded. She did like that story. She didn't have a story to say back. She of the fast lips. "Where's the food?" she said. The men laughed.

"Are you hungry?" Ivan's look was curious. Robbie wondered why she, the only person in the group with any fat on her body had to be the only who brought up food? Everest wore himself more serenely than anyone she had ever seen, tight-limbed, loose jointed. Even his features were finely drawn, a long thin nose, thin lips, thin eyebrows straight across his narrow brow from which straight hair was combed severely back. She felt like a turtle next to him and had she been one, she would have pulled her head inside and waddled away.

"No," she said.

"You won't be hungry again. If you eat you'll get sick." It was weird. A hot flush rolled through Robbie, like all this might actually be real. "Do you remember in the Bible the lilies of the field? How well they were cared for? In the park, we too are cared for. You can't eat, but you won't be hungry. You can't drink, but you don't get thirsty. You can't make yourself a permanent home, but you're fairly impervious to temperature and climate. Your needs are all attended to by eliminating them."

"That way you don't need to inflict yourself on the environment," Bart said.

"Pretty sneaky, huh?" Everest said. His chin dropped and his eyelids followed. "You got any plans for after the party?" Robbie knew he meant her.

"We're not sure yet," Ivan answered. "We'll be around." He took Robbie's elbow and drove her to the stairs. Midway down, he pressed his lips against her ears.

"How does it feel to be the belle of the ball?" The shock that stamped itself on her face was so stupid he laughed. "Honestly, what did you ever do without me? You're the hottest thing here. Everybody's after you. Can't you tell?"

Robbie thought: I should be home. My daughter is probably wondering where I am. Maybe she's crying because her mommy hasn't been home all day. How long it will be before she stops crying? How long before she forgets me? Robbie blinked hard. What could she do about it now? How dumb was it to go running late at night? Who did she think she was? Get beyond yourself and life smacks you back. If the devil had appeared in a puff of smoke she would have handed over her soul to be home, blowing raspberries on Paloma's stomach, smelling her soft skin, feeling her plump arms around her mother's neck. If you have not had a child, you do not know what physical love is.

Robbie looked down at the party a few steps below. Most of the heads near the staircase turned away. "They're only being polite. Every one of them would love to get their hands on you. You're nearly live. You're fresh. You're young."

Young?

"How young?"

"Barely legal." Ivan grinned.

How often had Robbie thought, "If I knew then what I know now..." How often had she stolen looks at girls fifteen years younger than she was, dining in expensive restaurants with men 10 years older than she was? Robbie wasted her own youth on boys who took her beauty for granted, as she had taken theirs. How had those girls gotten so smart? How had they known there was a heavy price they could extract for sharing their pretty company? Newly dead meant young here? Well, Robbie knew now what she didn't know then.

"Is this the whole community of dead people?" she asked. She thought perhaps there were forty or fifty there, but she knew she was bad at estimating crowds. And everyone kept moving.

"I prefer 'wraiths,'" Ivan said. "Much more elegant than 'ghosts', and not as ugly as 'dead people.'"

"Okay. Is this everybody?"

"Pretty much, not counting the Duchess."

"What about those boys near 103rd Street?"

"The Fauves could come if they wanted to," Ivan said. Robbie heard an air of injured innocence, like a WASP swearing it never occurred to him that there were no blacks at his country club.

Raul still stood in his spot, amongst a growing pile of presents. He had a gold pen, a paisley notebook, a silver comb, a stuffed doll. A watch hung loosely against his delicate wrist. Several chains hung from his neck. While Robbie watched, a slim woman with abundant hair dropped another chain over Raul's sleek head. A gold crucifix with a tiny ruby in the center. Robbie asked Ivan, "Can you introduce me to him?"

"I fall at your feet!" Raul screamed at her approach, his arms flung wide. He dropped to his knees. "I worship your walk." Robbie, who in life had despaired at her hips, who had suffered the embarrassment of trailing catcalls in her walk's wake, who had been a woman who took dance classes to learn how to not move, deigned to accept his adoration. At the party's end she left with Raul and his cache.

"Don't tell anyone where he takes you," Ivan whispered. "He'll be gone soon, and you can have his place. If you find a place to be private, don't give it away, to anyone. A lot of us are here for a very long time. Don't share your privacy. It's the same as giving it away. Are you listening to me?" Ivan held her hard with his off-temperature fingers. When Robbie'd been alive she'd had her bed to go to. She'd had a quilt with bits of bright and faded fabric sewn in a crazy conglomeration, no pattern, just shapes fitted together, but warm and comforting as hot tea toddy, steam rising. When she'd been alive she'd huddle under it and then all the new hurts in her mind, the unkind words she received, the shame she felt at the unkind words she'd said, her blanket would sop them up like a roll in gravy.

Raul slept in a hole in the ground whose opening was partly covered by tree root. Robbie wouldn't go in. They went back to the tree house and found a place on the floor not close to anyone else. Raul and Robbie hugged all night. He ran his hands along her arms, her legs, he smoothed her hair, he tended her like his lamb while she slept. When he died he'd spent his first night alone; he was glad to comfort a newbie and glad to feel her warmth.

At the sun's rising, Raul was floating on his feet facing Fifth Avenue, his chest bare, his pelvis covered by a belt of rope from which the trinkets he'd received the night before were suspended. Gold chains, pens, lockets, notes scribbled by those who could not write but could stuff their longing between the lines. Love makes all things possible.

"I'm going," Raul said. Above him, the sky opened like a choirboy's mouth and down bloomed garlands; irises and sprays of freesia, long ropes of flowers, and between each pair, a wooden seat painted like bits of rainbow, and on each seat sat an angel in a pale, colorless tunic that shimmered in the dawn. And as their slim legs pumped them into wider and faster arcs until their flight was a blur, Raul levitated, slowly revolving, his arms outstretched, his eyes filled with tears, a glory of light and smiles. The angels were singing, "It Don't' Mean a Thing if It Ain't Got That Swing," in voices like bells, tingly and effervescent. They all had Madonna, the singer's, face from when she was young, even the boys, with their tough, toothy smiles and their hair shaved close to their scalps. The swings formed a wide, bright circle, a perfect three hundred and sixty degrees of Maxfield Parrish poster, the middle of which was finally Raul, and the angels, their small torsos leaning back, their arms tight, bending the flower garlands where their tiny fists grabbed them, swung their synchronized swings toward that center and when they arrived there, they were gone with Raul. Nothing left of him but the sky that he'd disappeared into, hot pink and blue and quiet. Robbie waved.

Denial

Raul had given Robbie a pen and a small notebook. Robbie wrote in it. If she couldn't write after she was buried, then by God, she'd write before she was buried. Who was she writing for? If she passed her little book onto a living, she'd lose her future in Heaven. No way did she want to give that up. The deads couldn't read. So who was she writing for? For what? It was what she did.

Day 2, morning

I just saw Raul ascend into Heaven. Concept, casting, costuming, music, drama, climax – it was the most marvelous show I've ever seen, better even than fireworks. No one saw it, to my knowledge, but me. Where was everyone? Why was no one here to watch Raul enter another world? It was no secret that he'd be going, yet no one showed up to see him leave. Perhaps to see it and not go, to see the door open and not fly through is too painful. It must get old, being here.

Day 2, later

Rodrigo looks like a drug addict, skinny legs, unfinished tattoos of beasts of dubious mythological origins on his arms.

"What you got here," he says from the edge of the Bandshell stage, "you got your Buddhists, your Catholics, your Blacks, your gays, your brothers of Hispanic descent." I was heading down to Fifth and 59th, planning a Lewis and Clark exploration from the bottom up. Normally, I would have put a lot of space between me and a man who looked like Rodrigo, but the whole idea

is to record what's here and my reporter persona was intrigued.

Rodrigo has a keloid scar that winds its way from under his right ear to above his left nipple. The rest of his face is knotty. Juicy details.

"You ever been to the beach? Jones?" he says. "Good. You know how at Parking Field 2 they got these strips of territories? Families with their coolers and umbrellas and blankets and towels and kids in the center, nearest all the lifeguards, right opposite the building with the bathrooms and hot-dogs and stuff. Facing the ocean, you turn left. Walking along the water, first you get your couples, boys and girls, some of 'em with radios, not too loud though, some of them plugged together into their Walkmans. I think that looks cute, don't it? Then you got your Blacks. They get there early. By about one, two o'clock, they're history. They don't like to get too dark. Don't tell me. I know. I got Black brothers and a Black sister. They're the smart ones in my family. Me, I'm the good-looking one.

"After that you got your strip of nudies going topless, and then the fairies."

Right on the blurry edge of observant and offensive. He nods his head at our surroundings. "Now here you got your bloods uptown, same as in the city. Up by the Harlem Meer, around the Lasker Rink, they hang tough there. Couple of wiggers, too.

"The gays and yuppies like to stay down at the south end of the park. El Norte, it's like, wilderness to them. Not enough playgrounds. Not enough rollerbladers and moms and dads with strollers. The horse people, though, they like it uptown.

"You Jewish? I didn't think so, but you know, Sammy Davis, and then there are those Jews from Ethiopia, and the lost tribe. I know about that stuff, don't

look so surprised. I could be wrong, but I don't think there're any Jew spooks. Two reasons: You gotta die in the park to be a spook here. Jews don't die in the park. When they come, what could they die from? Heart attack while jogging or playing tennis, that's about it. Number two: To be a spook here you gotta love the park. To Jews, the park is mostly just a good view. Maybe it's okay to catch a free concert, or for a running track around the Reservoir, but as a place, hell, what's to love? Too many of us," he rubs his left forearm with a couple of roughened fingers on his right hand, "here.

"Latinos, we got a lot of us here. You, you don't got no group. Except maybe you'll be part of the loners group. And that's no group."

What I liked best about writing for magazines was it allowed me to skip past my inhibitions around talking to strangers. "I'm writing an article for Lear's," is an opening line so strong it bolsters confidence and confidences. In my reporter persona, I can hear neutrally, or at least, respond neutrally. My reporter personal didn't care that Rodrigo saw me as a loner with no group. Based on what evidence? He didn't know me. And I was kind of thinking of Ivan as my group. Or, as me as a member of Ivan's group, a chick snuggled under his wing.

Day 2, later still

Oh, my God! I'm not getting buried today! There's a gravediggers strike! Ivan heard it on a park maintenance worker's radio. And I know why. I'm going home. Thank you, God. Thank you. Thank you for my second chance. I've learned my lesson. Here is my joyous vow: I will live my life well. I won't hide my talents under a bushel, I won't scurry to the safe shadows, I won't be dishonest about my feelings. I won't be shy, or paranoid, or unwilling to take chances. I will value myself more. I will be the person I could have been.

I get it. Before this gravedigger's strike thing is settled, I'll be back home. I can see it happening:

INT. CASKET. DAY.
It is dark, with only enough illumination to discern the shape of a body on dimly shiny fabric.

CUT TO:

INT. WORKROOM. DAY.
Pull out to reveal a room with windows high in the walls. A dozen caskets in two rows crowd the room. UNDERTAKER, an elderly Black man in an ageless suit under a white apron, washes his hands at a deep sink by the back door.

SFX: A FAINT VOICE.

UNDERTAKER's eyebrows rise.

SFX: A FAINT VOICE.

UNDERTAKER
Who's there?

Dust floats in the sunlight through the windows. The caskets shine. All is still.

The Undertakes laughs at himself.

SFX: A FAINT VOICE.

Undertaker shuts off the water. He listens. He walks to the back door and opens it.

CUT TO:

EXT. BACKYARD. DAY.

The roses are full. The maple trees against the enclosing wall are heavy with leaves. Nobody's out here.

SFX: A FAINT VOICE.

CUT TO:

INT. WORKROOM. DAY
Undertaker turns back to the room.

SFX: A FAINT VOICE.

It's coming from the second casket from the door.
The UNDERTAKER steps to it and lifts the lid.

From inside, ROBERTA ROSE WILLIAMS, in a shirtwaist dress, sits up.

ROBERTA ROSE WILLIAMS
Thank you. Don't be frightened. I'm ready to go home now.

Day 2, afternoon

I'm going to have to get an early warning system for Ivan. A bell around his neck or something. Not touching the ground when you walk makes you silent when you ~~walk~~ glind. He just called me a lucky stiff. Funny.

Day 3

We livings are the wraiths' soap operas. The wraiths follow and eavesdrop on us as we walk through the park on our way to work or wherever. Whoever passes through the park on a regular schedule probably has, or had, a following. Ivan's into:

- *Courtney and Sky, two schoolgirls who talked about boys from Central Park West and 96th to Fifth Avenue and 95th.*
- *Manny and Elizabeth. From Central Park West and 102nd down to 59th and Fifth, Manny tried to get Elizabeth to tongue kiss him. She laughed as he talked about how fresh his breath was, this being morning and him being recently showered and toothbrushed. She laughed as he promised his shiksa wife would never know. She laughed as he told her about being a terrible lover, small penis, fast comer, but a great kisser. And very serious, she told him this wasn't fun for her at all, and couldn't they talk about something else? Manny switched to talking about Roger's foot fetish, and how Roger wanted to ask Liz for a pair of her old shoes, but was too shy.*
- *Dear Old Dishwater – Ivan's name for her – is the one he's been watching the longest. She's a woman that other women call older, not because of her age, which is probably early forties, but because of her style – utility without fun. Beige support hose, a walk without a hint of springiness despite her Nike's thick rubber soles and air springs. Ivan made fun of her, glinding backwards making faces in her face, doing a very credible imitation of her fast stomp. (He said he didn't do that to me when I was a living. I asked. He was putting on a show for me. I treasured it. I could tell he was glad he made me laugh.) Dear Old Dishwater doesn't have revealing conversation walking alone, plugged into her personal stereo,*

but she gives up details of her life all the same. She's a special case. Ivan says he used to feel sorry for her. Now she makes him mad. She never has a good time. She made me mad, too. When I get back, I'm not going to be like her. Ivan watches most of his soaps for a season or two before he switches to new ones. But he's gotten attached to a few. Dear Old Dishwater. And one he watched one from infancy until the boy went away to boarding school. Bartalemeo Mio. Ivan says he was a beautiful, naughty, funny little boy. I hope I get to see him. Ivan would like that.

Day 3, later

The Roman Catholic Church must run Heaven. They get all the best real estate.

I wonder how many Heavens there must be? Or else there's just one Heaven, and it's nearly empty. Crackers couldn't feel respected living eternally with niggras. Israelis would go berserk in a Heaven with A-rabs. Brits would petition if anybody else were allowed in. If people keep their personalities after they go to Heaven, and Heaven is a happy place, both of which I believe, then Heaven is either segregated, which I can't believe, or there are different Heavens for like emotional and intellectual disabilities. Or else hardly anybody goes. Mother Teresa. Gandhi. Martin Luther King, Jr. Me. Ivan.

Day 4

Ivan's friends are hitting on me. I don't like it. I feel like lunch. They all say "Let's be friends," but they're liars. Showing up with their offerings of gossip and secrets. They have agendas that don't match mine. I lay out my agenda, which is friendship, and they say okay, and then they go on with their agendas, which is get into my pants. Everest. He says we're friends, but then he grabs my hand while he tells me he's there for me. Friends don't kiss on the mouth, or hug and not let go. Friends don't invite me to spend the night, and then rub up against my back, and have the nerve to pretend they were asleep. What am I, stupid? I still have warmth in my bones; I walk and feel like I have a body on me. I told Everest he was a sneaky dog and not to let my name pass his lips again. I called Bart a little piglet. He does look like a pig with that squashed uptilted nose. When I was alive the first time I was too timid to say those things. I was all mealy-mouthed and considerate of the other person and worried about their dignity. Now I'm claiming my own and they can kiss my royal Black ass.

Ivan offered to fuck me when I lose my last warmth. He keeps spoon feeding me what to expect, how unpleasant it is. He's trying to help, but this is outside his experience. He doesn't understand that I'm going back to life.

Day 5

Every half hour from morning to early evening the animals come out and dance on the Delacorte Music Clock. In my entire life I took the time to see it less than half a dozen times. I do it more, now. Yesterday, me and a few livings watched the piping goat, the hippo violinist, the kangaroo playing his horn, the bear striking his tambourine, circling the clock, making their music. Among the livings with their faces up to the ringing clock was a family, mother, father, and baby daughter. I followed them.

The mother was short, no taller than my five-two, and the father about six-three, like John. The little girl was under two, round and gurgling. She wore lime green plastic jellies and a jumper over diapers. Her legs were Michelin Tire Man fat, fat enough to make you laugh and her smile was pink and round and she ran and looked back to make sure her mother was chasing her, then she'd laugh and run again. The father wore a large knapsack, mostly empty from the shape of it, and carried a bright red and orange striped blanket under his arm. He had an easy way he walked, kind of lazy, like what he was moving toward just might inch toward him if it got tired enough of waiting.

They settled on a little patch of green just north of Balto. Their blanket was spread, the baby slept, the mother lay down. The father lay beside her, curling his length to match her, snuggling his crown into the space between her ear and collarbone, cozy and pretty. She was angry about something. It was clear in her posture and fidgeting and the stiffening of her jaw.

"Did you put a dryer sheet in with this when you did the laundry?" she asked.

"I don't remember."

"You did. I can smell it."

"I don't remember."

"Well, you should remember. I'm allergic to that stuff."

"I forgot."

"You forgot, but I'm the one who doesn't have anywhere to lie down. I can't lie on the blanket. I'll start wheezing."

"Everything I do is wrong," he complained.

Why can't people be happy?

I love writing like this. Free. The words as fast or slow as they want. As hateful, disappointed or joyous as they want. My little book is full, both sides of each page, headings, margins, between the lines. The pages are thin and soft. I'm becoming a better writer. A much better writer. My writer muscles are pumping up. I can write circles around the writer I was.

It took a week for the strike to settle. Robbie knew the sour smell, like the sweaty crack of a lover with less than perfect hygiene, was herself she was sniffing. She was nauseous. She would have traded it for pain. Pain was sharp, and clear, or throbbing, pain had edges. This had no boundaries. It was like snot throughout her body. Like being wiped in snot, outside and in. Snot just slightly under room temperature. How long could this last, this nasty feeling on the verge of vomiting? Her breath was so bad she couldn't open her mouth. Her burps were the flavor of rotten eggs.

Robbie found Ivan hanging out on a ledge at Belvedere Castle with his friends. She didn't bother to move out of earshot to ask Ivan for his mercy hump.

"No," he said. "It's only the touching you need." The friends she had insulted - Everest, Bart, Simon, even Morrison who hardly ever said anything and certainly nothing to her, all of them joined Ivan holding her levitated, supported at her head and shoulders and waist and feet, passing her around in a circle, humming chatting, stroking her forehead, her chest and arms, holding her hands tight. Their hands felt less and less clammy and she felt more and more sick. A game started on the ball field; she could hear the smack of the bat and the suck of the air behind the ball, the cheers and groans of the crowd. The breeze that brushed them brushed her as well. She closed her eyes and the nausea intensified, she opened them and watched the sky rotate. Whichever she did was worse than the other.

When the group released her, her feet hovered inches above the ground, the tops of grass blades sometime brushing her feet. Glinding was only barely like walking, more like skating or rollerblading superfast and hypererect. She took off toward Fifth Avenue and smack into the wall. She was going to have to learn how to stop.

She dropped her notebook into a puddle and the words all washed away.

Summer

Unexpectedly, the park didn't contract over time. It sprawled from rocks to meadows, from gardens to glens, lakes to ball fields. For Robbie it was like the island of Jamaica. The lower end with its cafés and boating concessions and promenades and playgrounds and Bandshell and fountains was MoBay. Above about 79th Street the tourist destinations thinned and live and let live prevailed like in Ocho Rios and the locals weren't always there to help the tourists adjust and you could climb the waterfall without a guide. The upper end with the North Woods was Negril the way it was in the early seventies when there was nothing to do at night but make friends and get high. It grew familiar, the rock outcropping at West 106th Street, the hill from there to 110th, the ducks in the pond at 103rd, Strawberry Fields, (Did Yoko still live across the street?) the Bowling Green at 72nd. It was home. It was adventure. Robbie hadn't been an outdoor girl except for running. Now she got to see the streetlights go out and the sun rise up, to learn the names of the park workers. Avalon with his Jamaican accent. Jimmy straight outta Brooklyn. Serena. Neddie. Troy.

Before even the runners were out, when the sun was just turning the edges of the sky blue, Ivan liked to go out in the boats on the lake. He didn't take a boat if anyone was there and he was always certain to put the boat back exactly the way he'd found it. "The point is to keep ourselves secret and not impact on the lives of the livings. The point is not that we have a terrible time." Robbie was scared God would keep her out of Heaven if she used a boat. "Come on," Ivan said. The lake was smooth and silver as a polished tray. "Come on." Half expecting a clap of thunder, or at the least, a dead dove to drop from above, Robbie stepped out on faith and into the rowboat.

Out on the water is distant, even when the water is a manmade inland pond and only a few acres. The water is loud, the land noises fade, time floats. The rowboat drifted under a weeping willow and Ivan's impossible beauty slipped into darkness.

"My life was wonderful," Ivan said. "Not that there weren't struggles. I could tell you stories. Still, the struggles were wonderful, too. The tougher the time, the prouder I was of myself for coming through it.

"Want to play a game?" He raised his arched eyebrows.

"If you want." Soft light began to smudge the sky. She wanted to stay and she wanted to hurry back.

"It's called 'unwrap the good times'. Memories are gifts you can keep and share, too. Unwrap a memory and let me see it."

Robbie couldn't find a single appropriate memory. She wasn't trotting out her daughter, which was the best memory of all. Or her courtship. And if not those, what else was there? Her asthmatic childhood? Her years at elementary school as the only Black kid in the class? The birthday party invitations in their little white envelopes on everybody's desk but hers? Sophie Rothschild explaining, "I don't think you'd have a very good time." Or the beginning of that same year when she was fresh back from an August on her grandparents' farm and Herbert Klemienoff told her she had gotten a tan. Everybody laughed and somehow she was the joke. Her high school boyfriend dropping her a month before the prom because he knew she'd hold onto her virginity? What about the time, summer break after her freshman year in college when she'd left a party with a stranger who offered to walk her to her car, and they'd stopped off at his apartment for an umbrella and he'd raped her? He gave her his phone number, like they'd get together again. How about spending her last day losing the Bontemps and celebrating? She remembered the heat in her face, how much a fool she felt halfway between her chair and standing. Hardly fun things to pass around and exclaim over.

"Speak up." Ivan nudged her knee with his toe.

"I didn't have a wonderful life."

"But you miss it." He smiled, which erased the pain.

"I think I could have made it wonderful. I just hadn't yet," Robbie said.

Pink clouds were turning white in the east. Robbie liked this time; private and promising, the treetops developing detail. "Unwrap one of yours for me," she said.

"The first time I was called a bitch. Studio 54. I'd been allowed to help dress the girls for a Halston show. And after, Halston lent me a lavender jumpsuit. So I went home after working like a slave all day and looking how one looks when one is harried and sweaty and not grand at all. And I came back to the party fabulous. And Greta, the slave-driver saw me and screamed, 'You Bitch!' Greta acknowledged only the most dangerous competition. All night, everyone knew who I was. At fifteen."

Robbie never went to Studio 54. Skipped the whole thing. She'd had her days and nights of dancing, going roller skating at the rink at the old world's fair site in Queens, feeling the beat come up through the floor at The Garage, being let into a gay club down in a neighborhood that didn't have a name yet back in the day. Of taking a nap after work and then going out. Of cocaine at midnight and breakfast on the way home. Boogie oogie oggying 'till she just couldn't boogie no more. But Studio 54 was for famous people. For standing on line and letting an arbiter decide who was cool enough to get in. Robbie often quoted her friend Page's quip: "I only do entrance exams for B school." In retrospect, Robbie could see that she'd had the cuteness to get in, but not the courage.

All the rose and gold had left the sky.

"Time to get back," Ivan said. He pulled the oars. His biceps danced under his skin. "Every body of water in the park is fed by a pipe and operated by an on/off handle. Like giant bathtubs. On freezing days, the waterfalls don't run. Ever notice?" Ivan reached out for the closest boat. It was like the hand of Adam reaching to touch the hand of the Creator.

"I had an experience kind of like that," Robbie said.

"Where somebody called you a bitch?"

"Sort of. Where I was recognized. I caught somebody's boyfriend's eye. And she said she was going to beat me up. I didn't even know her boyfriend. But I felt this excitement 'cause there was buzz around me."

"And you liked it."

"I was ambivalent. I liked being recognized. I didn't like being recognized as a threat. Or whatever."

"Girlfriend. Didn't you ever hear that there's no free lunch?" The boat back in place, Ivan showed Robbie how to balance on its ribs as it rocked in the mild current.

"We're working on your core," Ivan announced, "Remember how your mother told you to get an education because that couldn't be taken away from you? Even Death can't rob you of what you know. I was a karate instructor. I'm going to teach you to kick the Fauves' asses.

"You look like a safe little target, but you're strong and limber." An advantage to having no blood was no blushing. Ivan went on, "So you can learn. Have to. You can't move through the world afraid."

"Better scared than scarred, I always say."

"No you don't. I'm never afraid. The closest thing I feel to fear is curiosity. Wondering how it's going to turn out. I swear, curiosity is the hook that reels people in to Heaven. Why else go? It can't be any nicer than this." He balanced the view on his hands: the Boathouse café, the sun through the weeping willows letting their hair down.

Ivan chose the center lawn of the Conservatory Garden for lessons. The garden presides at 105th Street, decorous as a young lady in a summer frock strolling under a wide-brimmed hat and a parasol. The long green lawn was well tended, quiet, and surrounded by crabapple blossoms in the spring. That summer it smelled of roses.

Ivan was a patient and demanding teacher, insisting on being addressed as Sensei during lessons. He had taught in Chinatown, he said, on the third floor of a derelict building. He could have overcome the men who killed him had he not been hampered by his trousers around his ankles. Ivan regretted rien. And he knew how to lead a workout.

He pushed her endlessly. Repetition after repetition. Combinations. Lifts. Ducks. Balancing. Sit-ups. Thousands of sit-ups. Pushups. Kicks and jumps. Higher. Faster. More. Again. How many times does one repeat a motion before the mind can wander while the body does its work? Robbie never found out. Every move was mindful.

The Fauves came down to watch her train, settling on the roof of the wisteria pergola, their hoots tumbling along the garden borders. Sometimes they came even closer, yelling their jokes from the top of the men's bathroom. The better she got, the more their derision encouraged her. She, who used to live on praise and shrivel on disapproval. She learned not to care and then not to notice. And then, bored probably, the Fauves stopped coming.

Ivan kept working her. After practices, Robbie was more tired than she'd ever been. Limp above the grass, her chest heaving, breathing, happy to feel alive and invincible. The leaves along the walkways grew thin. In the north garden volunteers emptied out the flower beds and put chrysanthemums in.

"You have to be able to disarm them if they come at you with weapons," he said, making her feel less ready and more motivated. She remembered their sharpened tin cans. Her speed multiplied many times over. Wraiths aren't stronger than livings, but they are so much faster their velocity makes it seem so.

When Ivan was satisfied Robbie could protect herself and vanquish others he sent her up to the Blockhouse. The Fauves hung out there, claiming the ruin as their own and passing time in it in ways similar to the War of 1812 soldiers who used it before them.

Napping. Scratching. Telling tall tales about their own bravery. Confessing their fears.

The Blockhouse tumbles on a tall hill near the 110th Street and Lenox Avenue entrance. From the fort, the boys could see the roofs of Harlem, and the traffic along 110th Street and Central Park West. If you know it's there, and you stand on the North Drive at 107th Street and look towards the Bronx, you can see it, its quiet colors much the same in winter as the naked trees that surround it. Four stone walls, no roof and a chained iron gate at the entry. A flag flies above from a pole inside. In the summer, except for that flag, the old fort is nearly invisible. To Robbie it seemed a desolate spot in the middle of nowhere. She arrived itching for a fight, but no one was there. It was all hers to wait in. Sitting in the silence she had time to question what she was doing. What was she fighting for? The intangibles with which heroes defined themselves. Pride. Honor. Bragging rights, for the less spiritually evolved. Whatever advantage being dead gave her, her adversaries had as well, and maybe even more so. She at least had the hopes of moving on from here. They were here forever. This was their place, like it or not.

Actually, she thought they liked it. She did. Dead in the park offered a Wild West kind of freedom. Sleeping under the stars. Watching other people go to work and not having to go herself. There was a sly pleasure in that, still. Then there was the interest and time and instruction Ivan lavished on her. Was she doing this whole thing to please Ivan? To continue her role as his star pupil? In life, she'd been a terrific student. It was after commencement, when the expectations weren't so clear, that she'd floundered. What to go after? Fame? That would have been nice.

Fortune. She had nothing against fortune, either. Love, happiness, respect?

Robbie sat in her hidey-hole watching the sweet, shy moon on its endless chase after the bright and glamorous sun. Did the moon ever catch up on the other side of the world? What was she doing, sitting here waiting for a bunch of boys to come try to beat her up? She watched the sky, listening to the soft crush of night animals on dead leaves and dry branches and damp rocks and grew nervous in the dark. What was she afraid of? Ivan had practiced her, sometimes with a blindfold around her eyes. She could cripple a group, she was sure. What about a group with weapons? Face-smashing broken bottles with necks for handles? Tin can lids sharpened like razors on rocks for as many hours as she had been sharpened on exercise?

"Beat them and you will never be threatened by them. You'll be free throughout the park," Ivan had said. But why not just avoid them? If they bothered her, then she could fight them. Why go looking? Why the showdown? By the time the boys came, Robbie knew why. It was for the rush.

When she heard pebbles fall from the wall above her, it was on. She felt the air condense as a body hurtled toward her. Duck left. Shoulder right. Hip right, heel back. Thowmp. She was grabbed from behind and lifted, eyes momentarily facing the sky. Focus. Knees together, up. Thrust out. Man down. Elbows back hard, head back hard. Contact. Dropped. Twist from oncoming foot. Yank the attached ankle. Jump up. Inhale. Exhale. Breathe. Chop down with palm. Clutch fist, hold tight, pull forward, slip behind. Ouch with birdsong backup. Hairy Upper Lip diving toward solar plexus. Leap up. Both hands on neck. Pull through open legs, push back. Spin. Chop to neck. Stomp. Step back, plant left, plant right. Ready, head dodging an imaginary blow which never came. Just the sound of limping footsteps, and a little laughter fading away.

God, right now felt good. The air was a gauzy pink veil over air that would soon sparkle, now still the mist, the mystery. The grass smelled like summer. Her cheeks were cool. Her sweatshirt was torn at the neck and a damp leaf clung to her collarbone. Her hair must be a mess. It was a long time since she'd thought about her hair.

She laughed. She laughed some more. Her chest heaved out short coughs of merriment. Air out, air in collided inside her, and hiccupped up sparkling laughter. This is exciting. This is fun. This is air. This is sun, this is wind in my lungs. This is delicious. This smells like victory. She laughed until she stood with her hands on her knees, gulping up big scoops of breath and choking. She spread out on the pebbly dirt.

Robbie was giddy with a revelation: Violence feels good. Once one could bring something besides fear to violence, it was da bomb. She asked herself why the discovery surprised her. Everybody decries violence. Everyone says that it's vile and evil and unnecessary. There's no way people would keep doing it unless it felt good. Given the right circumstances violence could be addictive.

The early sun was sweet on Robbie's head, the buildings on the West Side glowed warm as birthday candles. Hairy Upper Lip slipped sideways through the space in the bars blocking the door. Robbie watched him. She could fight some more. There was so much to fight about. The way the Fauves tried to -- okay, *did* scare her the day she arrived, when they could have met her with empathy. She could fight about that. She could fight about being damn dead. That would be a good fight. The overgrown boy came step stop step, his head down, his eyes on her, like hers on him. Her move. No one would judge her either way. It was her story to tell. She raised her hand, he pulled her up.

"I heard this story. About a Fauve who walked out of the park." Robbie was talking to the Fauve Martian Mikey. Ivan had been right. Now that she wasn't afraid of the boys, they didn't bother her. Sometimes they'd sit together and talk. Mostly Robbie and the boys would just wave in acknowledgement. Silent greetings before they lost sight of each other.

"Who told you that?" Mikey said. They were passing the time on the top of The Cliff, too far to hear the music from Lasker.

"Rodrigo."

"Dang. I didn't know the downtownies knew."

"You may as well tell me. If Rodrigo knows, everybody knows."

"Everybody knows everything in this dang place." Mikey rolled his eyes. "There was this Fauve named Tre, right? Who was fighting one day with his main man, Phil. They were boxing, just fooling around, right?, when Tre's dog came running up the Great Hill. The dog jumped on Tre so hard she knocked him down. Phil couldn't believe it because Tre was a ghost and this dog, Gristle, was alive. And she was wiping her tongue all over Tre's face and Tre was laughing and happy because he was glad to see Gristle and be with her and know that she was still alive because he figured his moms woulda put Gristle down. Pit bulls eat a lot. But Gristle was alive, dropping spit all over the place and it was so good to see her. Gristle acted like Phil wasn't even there. Even when Phil touched her, it was like she couldn't feel it. But she could feel Tre, you dig? Tre and Gristle rolled around together, a grown boy and his bad rep dog, happy as pigs in shit with each other. And then Gristle grabbed Tre by the shirt and pulled him down the side of the Great Hill and out Stranger's Gate. Phil watched them go across 106th Street.

"That was the end of Tre in Central Park. Some people thought that Phil had hacked Tre up and buried him or something. Which was impossible." Mikey shook his head at the craziness of people.

"Once you eliminate the impossible, whatever remains no matter how improbable, must be the truth," Robbie said.

"You like Sherlock?" Mikey squeaked.

"Like Sherlock? I love me some Sherlock!" They grinned at each other over this mutual interest like strangers on a surprising good first date.

After a while, Mikey said, "Phil swore he was telling the truth.

"You know," he said, "before that happened, I heard that if you had true love, the kind of love that nothing could break, and was pure and true no matter what; if you had that kind of love with someone, you could leave the park alive if the person you had that love with came and got you. That person that you loved with all your heart and who loved you the same way could take you back to life out of the park."

Robbie wondered who loved her strong enough to bring her back from the dead? Who had that much loyalty? Who had unalloyed, ever-consistent love for her? Human beings weren't like that. Dogs could be like that, but people? No. Robbie wished she'd had a pet. And not just those stay-in-the tank fish that she never fed anyway. She'd left them for a week and a half without food once on a trip to L.A. back before she was married, and came home fully expecting to see neon tetras floating on the surface. Instead they were swimming silently, unaware that she'd even been gone, living off the algae growing in the tank. Thereafter, she didn't even bother to clean the tank or change the water. The fish were just her rent-free tenants. They weren't coming to the park to get her out of death.

Mikey went on, "When I heard it, it made me sad. I ain't never loved nobody like that. Thought I did. But then they'd do something to let me down, and I'd feel different. And then, even if she wanted to patch it up, I couldn't let it go back to the way it was. Too hard for my own good." Mikey laughed and hit his chest with his fist two times.

Robbie asked, but Martian Mikey didn't know what happened to Tre after he left. "How would I know? He never came back." Robbie didn't really need it spelled out. If she bumped into a living she loved, unconditionally, and that living loved her, unconditionally, she could have her life back.

But Robbie hadn't ever loved anyone unconditionally. Had she? Had she? Not her actor husband still reading for parts he'd outgrown because "that's where the money is. Once you play out of that range, you can't step back in. It's not an age thing. It's an image thing." She heard him say it, and thought to herself he could call it a career move if he wanted, but it was really ego and that he wanted to play the pretty roles. Unconditional love didn't think like that. Robbie had been on the outs with everyone in her family at one time or another. There was no one whose love didn't have the blot of a flaw or two or eleven, no one whose kindness she accepted as pure and free. She was well aware of the costs, down to the last emotional penny, the false compliment, the bitten tongue. There was no one for whom she felt love no matter what. Was there? Was unconditional loving even a capacity she had? And if unconditional love was reciprocal, there was no one from whom she might reasonably expect it, either. Except. Except.

Paloma. When Paloma cried for no reason, or wanted to be held in the middle of the night, or smeared indelible ink on the leather couch, Robbie loved her. Had she ever made a move toward or had a thought about her daughter that wasn't from love? No. Could she ever? No.

Just so you know, when someone dies it isn't just the livings that regret the things they never said or didn't say enough. The dead have the same regrets. Martian Mikey's story told Robbie death isn't stronger than love. Robbie believed that. So she took her love for her mother, her father, her sister, her brother, her husband and child, for the friends she'd harbored ungenerous thoughts about and strapped that love on a mental plane and sent it to them. Perhaps they felt a love surge that day. She couldn't tell. And then she closed the lid on that box and sat her butt down on top. That's it. No more. Time to bury that coffin and move on.

Only she couldn't completely. When she asked Ivan about it he sucked his teeth. "Believe what you want to believe," he said, and sighed. "And consider the messenger."

The Duchess didn't know anything except that love was a foolish indulgence and Robbie should know better. Better to put your faith in what you could touch and sell if you needed to.

Connivance

Ivan careened around the Swedish Cottage and snatched Robbie. He didn't wait for her to explain that she liked to watch the puppet shows and wanted to stay until the end of Cinderella. "We should hurry." They nearly flew uptown past the tennis courts and east to the little sand beach on the banks of the Meer. "Look."

It was a dead man. Robbie didn't usually like beards, but she liked this man's. Neat, luxurious, shining. She didn't usually like large men, either. Her gut reaction to large men was fear, but not with this one. This man didn't scare her at all, even over two hundred fifty pounds and over six foot five. And he was dark, a coffee with no cream whatsoever. His skin was unblemished, thanks in part she thought, to the beard. His cheeks were not roughened by years of shaving, pitted by bumps from ingrown hairs. It's funny – funny interesting, not funny haha -- how a feature so masculine as a beard gave him skin like a girl's. She liked the dichotomy. He looked to be about forty, maybe, so Robbie guessed he was about fifty, on the black don't crack tip.

"Nice, huh?" Ivan whispered.

"Yes." More than nice.

Back before Robbie and John married, before even they were engaged, they came out as a couple living in sin by inviting Robbie's parents to dinner in the apartment Robbie and John shared. Robbie's parents knew John and thought him nice enough but not good enough. And that he was unscrupulous to cohabit with their gullible daughter without benefit of marriage. That he was not steadily employed did not go in the plus column, either. Mommy and Daddy didn't have a lot to say over the dinner table. John jumped into the silence with one of the *Times* articles he was always finding about black people. Robbie herself skipped to the arts pages, but John would find news about black people and bring them to Robbie's attention. At some point she felt, "enough already;" his greater interest in black news made her feel . . . irresponsible. That night he had an article from the day's metro section about a man who kept young men out of jail by finding them jobs. John read it aloud in his beautiful, trained voice and passed it around the table. All dutifully looked at the pictures of the man, his arms around a couple of teenagers at a some rich family's reno in Greenwich Village. It got a conversation between the men that carried on past dinner. Normally a quiet woman, Robbie's mother took little part. But later, drying dishes while the men were up on the roof checking out the view, Robbie's mother had asked her: "Why couldn't you choose a man like the one in that article?"

This was that man.

Ivan said, "He bled to death. Attacked by four boys in the dark. I saw them sauntering away. Laughing. They didn't act like they were worried about getting caught." Robbie was both sad and ashamed.

The man's eyelids fluttered. His eyes were brown, faint wrinkles spread around them as he squinted. He saw light, blocked some by two faces. A woman. A prim set to her mouth. A questioning look around the eyes. He'd seen that questioning look on his boys' faces. The mouths would be saying, "Whadja looking at," while their faces wondered, "What do you see?" Kids whose bad diets showed in their bad skin, their bodies that were too fat or too thin. People saw the cheap dental work and the expensive sneakers. What the big man saw was potential for which he had to provide a chance. His name was Massimo.

Only the one name. It had been the name he used conversing with his mother and taking to the press. The one he used to sign the endless grant proposals and the countless letters of introduction he wrote to get his boys jobs. To get them out of the courts and into something more promising than jail. Massimo's goals were small if you already had better; if your dad could give you a job for the summer. If you were spending sophomore year learning French at the Sorbonne. For Massimo, success was a job for one of his boys at a car repair shop, a printing shop, part-time with Kinko's was fine if he could get it. Part-time with Kinko's could lead to two part-times, full-time, a manager's position. Massimo's boys had had successes and every year they were achieving more. Who knew what could happen, given time.

"I don't have any more time, do I?" he said.

His question came out nearly a song in an Old Man River voice. It rumbled around in his deep chest, picking up decibels like hitchhikers so that by the time it came out his mouth it sounded as if it had been places and learned things.

The man knew the effect of his size and his voice on his boys, on women, on other men. He enjoyed it. He used it well, to do good. It had taken him some time to get control of that body. At first the body had been too big for him; he'd been awkward and shy when he started growing. His mother could show you pictures: Massimo, long arms, long legs, knobby elbows and knees, big hands, even bigger feet. Massimo in an out-of-date tuxedo, his hair in a lumpy Afro, holding a corsage in a clear plastic box. Uncool Massimo before he'd gotten used to being in his body. But how could a boy get used to a body that refused to fit into the clothes that had fit last month? When the loose jams of June are tight shorts at the end of August? It took all four of his years at Harvard, but by commencement, Massimo was perfect.

Muscles were only the most obvious of his blessings. He had inspiration, vision, patience. He started his career on Wall Street, in the alleyways of big money, plenty swagger. He was good at it. Like all of that tribe, he collected unopened boxes of flat screens, and Bose speakers, 600 thread count sheets still in their wrappers, all that expensive fresh newness mixed with the squalor of unemptied trash in the kitchen in a harbor-view apartment that he was hardly ever in. He even showered at the gym downstairs at work, slipping into one of the shirts delivered from the laundry and kept by the half dozen in the bottom drawer in his cubicle.

Massimo left finance following his heart to Chambers Street, the courthouses. He found happiness pulling black boys from the mouth of the ravenous criminal justice system. The boys led him away from Chambers Street and on to City Hall. Still, it wasn't the corridors of politics he loved. He loved the potential in his boys.

"I was somewhere between a garbage picker and a gardener," he said later to Robbie. "I took the plants with bent stems and broken leaves, that had been stepped on, or didn't get enough sun or water or food, and I tended them. Staked them to give them backbone until they were strong and straight on their own."

Quitting his good jobs for increasingly less glamorous, less well-paid ones made Massimo an object of both pity and admiration among his former classmates and coworkers. They kept their ears open for mailroom jobs and painters' helper positions. One, who was having his new condo gutted, forced his contractor to take one of Massimo's boys as an apprentice carpenter. Juan. Turns out, Juan had a talent not for carpentry, but for talking with clients, and he stole only a little, much less than the union men on the job. The building trades have been in a downturn recently, but the contractor said he'd use Juan on his next job. One of Massimo's successes.

Massimo expected to be convincing to boys who expected to be lied to and who prided themselves on not being taken. Massimo could turn them with his dreams of them. When a group of four boys of great potential stabbed him he was mildly surprised, worried that he'd lost touch, and worse, fallen in love with his own image.

The other face leaning over Massimo was peaceful and gentle. Too beautiful for a man, although it was clearly a man's face. "My name is Ivan. How do you feel?" Massimo heaved himself upright to sit. He rotated his shoulders. Stretched his arms up overhead. Bent each of his fingers then straightened them out again.

"Great." Massimo continued his examination, his pleasure and puzzlement increasing. "I'm curious. This isn't what I expected at all. It's disappointing, but comforting, too. The definition of familiarity, huh?" When he finished speaking, he shut his mouth. As if he were giving reporters time to get it down right. He felt his back, took off his jacket, a soft, nubby tweed with shots of bright blue, and reached for the places he'd been stabbed. His shirt was a yellow balanced between baby chick and egg yolk. "I haven't been able to reach the middle of my back in years."

"You're more flexible after death," Ivan said. "It has something to do with gravity, I believe." The black man unbuttoned his creamy yellow shirt and took it off.

Ivan grinned outright at the depth of Massimo's chest. Robbie tried to take her eyes off the 'toids and the six pack, but they kept straying back.

"If they stabbed you in the ass, would you moon us?" Ivan winked. The Black man was apparently used to hecklers. He ignored Ivan.

"My shirt's not torn. No tears in my jacket, either." He looked up. Robbie snatched her gaze back to Massimo's face. "I know I got stabbed in the back, but my back feels fine." He carefully fingered the skin of his back, his nails darkly rosy against the black muscles.

Ivan went on, "Welcome to the afterlife. You loved the park and died in the park which makes you one of us."

Massimo accepted this quietly. Then he said, "So the little buggers got me. That's what comes of being cocky."

"I know who you are," Robbie said. "You rebuild brownstones with young ex-offenders. There was a story about you in the *Times*." She didn't mention how she'd heard about it.

"They did a few stories about me. The program, I mean. Yeah." The mouth shut again. He was so *there*. Like a tree trunk. Robbie pictured herself a big, itchy bear wanting to rub up against him and scratch herself good.

"I'm Robbie." And you're the sexiest man I've ever seen.

"You've got that vegetarian skin," he said. She smiled. She knew how she looked with his admiration all over her. Her skin turned on, her hair thicker, livelier, shinier. Her muscles more articulated. To herself in his dark eyes, she looks scrubbed and buffed and well-fed on ambrosia.

"I was a vegetarian," she said. She turned to Ivan. "Looks like you'll have competition in the handsome pageant."

"I have a weak chin." In the moment, Massimo admits it freely. He knows the magnanimous way he says it is misleading. He says it like one of those answers to the interview question: "What is your biggest fault as a manager?" And you answer something like, "I push myself too hard." BS. Massimo hates his chin. It ends too short, and worse, in a point, like a kitty cat's.

In the moment, Robbie thinks he's being modest. She doesn't imagine for a moment the truth.

"Well." Ivan did his best third wheel, and started to roll away. "Robbie will acquaint you with what's what. I'll introduce you to more people later."

"I do pretty good meeting people on my own." Massimo said, shutting his mouth at the end of the sentence.

"Let me introduce you to The Duchess. At least." Ivan said.

"Is she rich?"

"Fabulously."

"No more meeting rich people for me. I'm through."

"Oh, come on." Ivan beamed a full blast of hot charm.

"What's in it for you?" Massimo said. Not for nothing had he spent decades negotiating. His antennae were sharp to trading.

"She pays me for introductions."

"What?" Robbie couldn't believe it. Except she did. And it disturbed her. Why did it matter? He could have told her. She imagined him saying, "You didn't ask." And he'd be right. Massimo had asked and Ivan had told him. If Ivan had confided on that first day, "The

Duchess pays me for introductions," would Robbie have refused to meet the Duchess? No. She wanted to. She didn't know anybody. She was grateful. So now, why did she begrudge Ivan getting a benefit from the introduction? Did she? No. So what, then, bothered her? That he had secrets. But no, he didn't. What bothered her was that there were things about Ivan that she didn't know, and some of them concerned her directly. But wasn't that true on her side as well? Did she share every thought she had about Ivan with Ivan? Didn't she sometimes make (slight) fun of his hair toss to amuse a Fauve? She did. Thinking of it, (of them, for she'd done it more than once) she had the decency to lower her eyes. Did she tell Ivan everything? Of course not. He didn't tell her everything either. Robbie knew Ivan exposed his secrets more than she did.

It was jealousy. Pure and simple. Well, simple.

"She pays me. No one can stand her. I mean, you've met her."

"I can live without her," Massimo said, buttoning up his shirt.

Ivan kept explaining to Robbie. "She's convinced that to introduce herself to anyone gives them the upper hand. So I bring you to her. She gets to maintain the illusion of being presented to. Once I bring her thirty people, she'll let me choose any of her emeralds I want. Of course, I'm going to take the biggest one. I can't wait to watch her struggle to let it go. But a promise is a ---"

"What number am I?" Robbie interrupted.

"Twenty-seven," he said without hesitation.

Straight away, Robbie took Massimo to the Fort. All the Fauves were there. Billy. Exo. Little Bill. Martian Mikey. Phillip. Jeffrey, who Robbie had stopped thinking of as Hairy Upper Lip, and the white twins, Benjamin who they called Ben-jammin', and Steve, who had been potheads and knew how to hang and be chill. She introduced them at the Fort, liking the way her status in the Fauve's eyes elevated as she presented this big black man and he took over. It was nearly magic the way he engaged the boys; they talked about cellphones and beepers, confessed to loving baths, they made signs in a secret male language of half smiles and ellipses. Robbie watched them splash in the pond below the little wood bridge south of The Ravine. They shouted for her to come in too, but she shook her head no and congratulated herself on giving Massimo a seamless transition.

Massimo, dead, was still in his element, already thinking that perhaps he could get these wild ones a chance. He had a soft spot for Jeffrey, too young for his body, the way Massimo himself had once been, awkward in all that flesh and bone and boner. Exo was smart, the smartest of the group, trapped with them, and in this place with no outlet for his thinking. He was the most dangerous. Little Bill the dreamer, was a hazy thinker. He wanted a hero, an adult who cared.

Massimo wondered what the relationship between Ivan and Robbie was. Massimo's gaydar beeped high on the upper register with Ivan, but something beyond platonic buzzed between Ivan and Robbie. Something almost filial. Massimo had met a lot of people and he'd developed an expertise at reading them. He could see that Ivan felt responsible for Robbie, and that Ivan liked it. Massimo would have to see if Ivan would be interested in mentoring Little Bill.

In the afternoon the Fauves drifted in one direction, Robbie and Massimo in another.

"You say these boys can't go to Heaven? Because they've interfered with living beings?" Massimo said.

"Yeah." Robbie lingered at the edge of the road that runs between the East and West Drives at 102nd Street. "None of them that I've asked even remember what they did. They were just goofing. Moving livings' backpacks, silly stuff like that."

"That's not fair."

"I guess the line has to be drawn somewhere."

"Any line that's drawn can be erased."

"Depends, doesn't it, on what you draw it in?" Robbie put a pin in a thought: was a line in the sand more determined than a line drawn in blood? "And how many people went down crossing or defending it."

They followed the path across the West Drive and down the hill to the Duck Pond. Near where Robbie had first met the Fauves. What a frightened creature she had been then. "It's not fair to the boys to give them hope for something they can't have."

"God loves us. God wants us to be happy. Forgiving us makes God feel good," Massimo said. Robbie hoped it was so, but she wasn't holding her breath.

Massimo would maybe never be aware of it, but he loved the idea of getting the boys into Heaven maybe more than he thought he might come to love Robbie. Because he liked her right away, in that way that you like a place that feels like home. Robbie was like the girls who lived down the street on Williamson Avenue in Queens where Massimo grew up. Girls who had no idea how beautiful they were even though they thought they did. Girls who smoothed their eyebrows with spit-moistened fingers. Girls like his sister who sat on their beds at night talking on the phone while they rolled up their hair on pink sponge rollers and screamed at their little brothers to stop spying on them. Girls who kissed with their mouths shut. Robbie brought back memories of how exciting that was. She looked like summer to him. A summer in which legs lengthened and thighs thickened and armpits embarrassed. Playing hide and seek and catching lighting bugs. Her voice was like the evening of a long day.

They wandered north again, back to the Meer.

"I kept visiting where I died, too," Robbie said. "I wonder if everybody does that?"

"How did you die?"

"I got hit by a car," she said. He didn't disturb the silence with questions about how it felt and then what happened? She liked that he could think and not speak.

The sky turned purple. A breeze rippled the pond. "Are you cold?" Massimo said, and draped his jacket around her shoulders. Smooth, heavy silk lining against her shoulders. That's when her heart burst open. Right there, maybe half a day into their meeting. This was the guy her mother would have picked out for her. "Jesus," as the mothers quipped, "in a three-piece suit." She did not want to blow this.

"Yellow looks good on you," he said. It did. She didn't even tell him about not getting cold. She accepted his kindness. They stood hearing the traffic's hum, the drifting conversations around them, the water lapping against the stones, feeling the orange sun paint their faces. The color from his shirt reflected on the underside of her chin.

Robbie knew she was in dangerous territory. She'd already taken the man under her wing instead of letting him make the first move. He probably thought that she didn't want to dance the dance. She would have to let him know that he'd gotten the wrong impression.

"Thank you. You hold on to your jacket. You won't get another. Besides, once we're buried, the temperature has to be extreme for us to feel it." She shook his hand, wished him well and hid her wish for a kiss and left him standing by the Meer.

Massimo was a passionate man, but not a romantic one. He had no game. None. Unless following that timeless advice, "Just be yourself," counts. He knew to bring flowers and be polite to the mothers and dads, but by the time he could date seriously, he didn't need game. With his presence and education and access to the working wealthy, Massimo had gotten scooped up by the Alpha Girls early in life, which is the best thing that can happen to a serious young man. Alpha Girls are the girls who go to the best colleges, hairdressers and parties. Polished and confident, they believe in the best for themselves. They're friendly, competitive but grudge-free. If you manage to beat them at something, they still like you. They stay in touch with every useful contact they ever make. All Alpha Girls are related, sistered and networked together through blood or sorority or workplace/church/children's private or magnet school. Massimo was initiated into Alpha Girl rotation; evermore the girls moved him between them in the way of their tribe, and he never pursued a one. Like himself, they were suckers for potential.

Robbie hadn't been an Alpha Girl. She did not have the forwardness, or the expectation that any man she was interested in would return that interest doubled. She needed for Massimo to dance the dance with her, to do all the steps in the right cha-cha-cha.

Step one. The boy asks the girl for a date.

It was Ivan who gave Massimo the lay of the land and helped him through the transition at burial. The two men made a little event of it with the Fauves. "Rebirthing," Massimo called it, and the boys were his midwives. Massimo hadn't been so vulnerable or received such intense care since childhood. Sharing his need bonded the big man and the boys forever. Robbie kept herself scarce. She did not want his neediness to be a part of their story.

"I practically dropped this gorgeous hunk in your lap," Ivan said to Robbie, "and you tossed him back like he was a fish under the weight limit."

"I'm busy." Robbie was vague. Certainly, her schedule was not overburdened. Although it was obvious that she was spending more time on her hair.

Ivan repeated to Robbie what The Duchess said to him. "The Duchess told me that Massimo's made her consider going native." Stirring the pot. "It's the naughtiest thing I've ever heard her say." Robbie's head jerked up. "I told her she wasn't his type."

"Really?" Robbie had to ask, "What's his type?"

"You know what his type is."

"No, I don't. I don't know him," she said.

"Oh, please. I'm tired of you two talking to me about each other." He smiled his misleading angelic smile. "I want to get back to talking about me."

"What does he say about me?" Robbie suspected that Ivan enjoyed being the go-between.

"You're the kind of girl he respects. Good head on your shoulders, blah, blah, blah. And you're beautiful, but you don't act like you know it. High school stuff like that.

"I don't know why you two don't just do it. . .you haven't seen him since the day he got here, and there's no way that can happen by accident."

Robbie adjusted a skirt she'd twisted together with fallen leaves and blossom petals. These things lost their freshness before the day was over but they achieved an antique grace quickly and were nice even as they disintegrated. "If he wants to see me he can come find me." Robbie's playa move. She knew Ivan would run back and tell Massimo.

Massimo asked Ivan, "So. Did you see Robbie today?"

"Yes."

"What's she up to?" Massimo was showing his hoodlum boys how to tie and mold leaves into nests. He made a mixture of dead leaves and water and patted it into crisscrossed sticks until there was enough to attach to another piece. It needed the right mix of water and dirt and time. Manipulate the mixture too long and it didn't work; the leaves dissolved to powder and the compound fell apart. He was the first one to teach them anything.

"Oh, the usual. Glinding around. Spying on the livings. Moping about you." Ivan dipped his finger in the mud and drew polka-dots on his forearms.

"About me?" Massimo said. "I find that hard to believe." This was just pretending.

Massimo may have been game-free (or romance challenged), but the Fauves were wise in the ways to get girls.

"You got to take her something, Man."

"Like a book, or a flower, or you know, something you made."

"I don't know how to make anything like that," Massimo said. The idea of building a nest for himself and Robbie made him grin. That would be a big nest; but not much bigger than the nest he'd build for himself. It was summer and the leaves were thick.

"You know how to make a poem." Pronounced "Poe M."

"That's some bull, anyway," Exo said. "What women like is to talk. Ask her about herself."

The next day the Fauves let Massimo know that Robbie was hanging out at the Castle and that's where he found her. She felt his shadow and knew when she looked up, he'd be there. She arranged her face accordingly, lips slightly parted, eyes widened, careful to keep her eyebrows from rising.

"Tell me what made you happy?" he said. She was sitting on the ledge watching the crowd gather for Shakespeare in the Park. Kevin Klein and Andre Braugher and Ruben Santiago Hudson were performing *Measure for Measure.* Robbie had seen it the night before when the heat had been record breaking, and the audience grateful for the dark when it came bringing cooler temperatures with it.

Robbie thought about what made her happy. One afternoon on Fire Island when she was in her twenties. A tea dance. She'd gone with a group of housemates. They'd taken over the room, dancing alone, with each other, with others. And another time, on a motorboat back to Paros from the beach, sleepy, smelling her own sweet sweat, resting her eyes behind large sunglasses. She was skinny then; she remembered the hollows beside her hipbones and above her knees. Her shoulders rose and fell in time to the American tunes coming from the radio on the boat in the Greek sea. Sunk in sunlight, drunk on music.

"Dancing," she said.

It was summer, it was Sunday. Burning Spear playing at Rumsey Playfield. Robbie and Massimo went dancing.

Step Two. The boy declares himself.

After the concert they wandered up to Lasker Pool and crawled under the entry gate and stood close enough to the pool to get splashed. Delicious. Kids screaming, music on top, Bruce Springsteen, Naughty by Nature, Luther and Anita, teenagers cool by the pool, eyeing each other, the girls with their nails impossibly long and decorated like kimonos, the boys, long legged and long backed, hopping when they walked. There was sweetness to them. The little sisters and brothers the teenagers were supposed to keep an eye on dunked each other and got water and noise all over the place.

"I never came here when I was a living," Robbie said. "I missed out."

"You're kidding."

"No. I never went to any city pools."

"But you lived only a few blocks away. Didn't you ever just want to take a dip? Did you swim?"

"Did you?" She pushed him in. He rolled to avoid a fat kid barreling down on a skinny kid with a shaved head. Massimo climbed out.

"Thanks. I needed that." He knew flirting when he saw it.

"Every Sunday a group of us from high school went to the pool at Jones Beach. I had a crush on a boy, Billy, my first true love. That summer all the radios played 'Last Dance," and "Three Times a Lady." Robbie sang a little, "You're once, twice, three times a lady." Massimo nodding in time.

"The Commodores."

"I could make myself cry listening to that song. Anyway, Billy had a car and I would finagle myself into his car for the ride out to Jones. We always went to parking lot 4 where the pool was. One day I jumped off the diving board, a group of us were doing it. I couldn't dive, but I jumped. And I was proud of myself for doing it because the only other time I'd gone off a diving board the lifeguard pulled me out. So, I'm feeling good walking the length of the pool in my little bikini. And when I got to Billy, one of the girls, Shirley Enoch, pulled me aside and pointed to my breasts. My top had ridden up and one of my boobs was out. I was so embarrassed. I knew Billy would never like me after that."

"Probably made him like you more," Massimo said. He was probably right. Billy was Robbie's boyfriend through senior year in high school and on into freshman year at college. Still, the embarrassment of that afternoon long ago lay on Robbie as she and Massimo wandered downtown, in and out of the shadow and the sunlight. He lifted her over streams, held back branches. When they arrived at the Ladies Pavilion she suggested they sit on the roof. One thing about Mass, one small thing; in anything with a roof over it, Mass was so big Robbie felt crowded by him. In the outside, against the trees or sky or skyscrapers, Mass felt to her like a place she could burrow in a storm. Inside, he took up a lot of room.

"Don't be sad. Don't be sad about that guy," Massimo whispered to her. "You'll make me jealous. I don't want to be a jealous boyfriend. It's not a good look for me."

"Who said you're my boyfriend?"

He held her hand and her heart floated.

"That was a good summer. *Last Dance* by Donna Summer. *Miss You* from The Stones. And what about *Flashlight*?" Massimo hummed the baseline, bobbing his shoulders to the beat. He started singing. "Flashlight. Red light, Neon Light. Stoplight."

"Don't tell me you don't remember it, girl." Massimo grabbed her waist and pulled her into the rhythm.

"Everybody's got a little light under the sun, under the sun," she sang.

". . . under the sun," he joined in.

On the hill above them the Fauves looked at each other and grinned.

Step three. The girl returns his affection.

"Is this love, is this love, is this love, is this love that I'm feeling?" Robbie had reggae in her mind. Sometimes it was Bob Marley, sometimes it was Inner Circle. *"Love is a drug. Love, love, love."* Her step was quicker, her heart was quicker, her smile was quicker. She felt like superwoman.

How lucky could a girl get? What are the chances someone so perfect would show up right while Robbie was there to meet him? She could have met him while she was alive, but she hadn't. They could have been in the same bookstore at the same time or at the same parties. She might have met him through her husband who sometimes worked in an after school acting workshop. And then, this love wouldn't have happened. Isn't afterlife funny?

Robbie knew she hadn't gotten love right, witness the few – actually, the one – she could count with whom she shared unconditional love. This time she tried her hardest. She was organized in her thinking, making

lists, boiling down, eliminating redundancies, until she had her own constitutional framework from which to work. A set of criteria, if you will, living and open to interpretation but with the basic bedrock firm.
The 4 P's: Robbie's Rules of Love

> #1. Privacy. What happens in the love stays in the love. Neither lover shall expose private details to others. It's a matter of loyalty. No telling others that Robbie has bad breath when she wakes, or farts like a man, or is scared of strange noises. No sharing what Massimo shares with her alone – his secrets are safe in Robbie.
>
> #2. Publicity. "Secret" and "love" are not words that go together well. ("Pas des mots qui vont très bien ensemble," in the language of love.) Love grows in public. Friends, neighbors, family members – society is the sunshine and the rain that makes a coupledom strong. Attention and expectation from a wide group is fertile soil for romance. As well as they are poison for romances on the side.
>
> #3. Previous Priorities. Both parties are allowed his or her interests without complaint. If he loves golf, she can't begrudge him his golf time – so long as he shares meaningful time with her. If she meditates the very first thing in the morning, he can't throw his arm around her waist and push his pelvis against her hips when she wakes up. You have to be allowed to be who you are and do what you do; otherwise, it's not love; it's control. Control can be addictive, but it's only satisfying in spurts, and you're always sorry you participated.
>
> #4. Protection. This is the rule upon which all the

> others rest, the rule to which all the others are simply subsets. The lover will not hurt or let others hurt the beloved.

Robbie discussed these rules with Massimo early on, because in a relationship communication is key and setting expectations is necessary even if they seem obvious. Massimo listened and nodded and rubbed her head because he knew she liked having her head rubbed. He knew because she told him and he listened.

They discovered that his nest was big enough for the two of them, and Robbie always came to it freshly prettied up. Massimo, too, when the Fauves stared mentioning how much better Robbie was looking.

Massimo slept with his eyes open. The first time Robbie awakened in his arms and saw his open eyes, she'd been overcome with a love that was adolescent in its intensity and self-centeredness. She felt beautiful knowing he was watching her in her sleep. She kissed him. He brushed it away as if her kiss had been a fly and she realized he was sleeping. Spooky. Robbie watched the rise and fall of his chest. The dark eyelashes. The quiet way he shifted, carefully, as if he didn't want to hurt her, as if even asleep he was aware of her, valuing her. No one Robbie had ever known was as gentle as Massimo or as committed in deed to his beliefs. If he thought it was wrong, he didn't do it. If he thought it was right, he did. "Are you absolutely perfect?" Robbie whispered into his armpit, her fingers tracing his rippled stomach.

Robbie created an affair around herself and Massimo that was like a garden. It flourished in the spotlight of love. Proof of Robbie's Rule #2. People wanted in, and visit they did, but Robbie's Eden belonged to the Robbie and Massimo alone. Proof of

Robbie's Rule #1. She giggled at jokes nobody else understood. She winked when they were too far apart to kiss. Even when they were not together, she noticed the world around her more sharply; she brought back souvenirs to share. "Did you see the rainbow this afternoon? I was hoping you were looking at it when I was. I thought of you."

Robbie and Massimo. When they were apart she rehearsed what she would say when she saw him again. Struck poses. Practiced to look and be her best. For that is what love does for us. It makes us put our best selves forward.

Their affair never cooled to the point where Robbie could look at Massimo without feeling like she was blushing. He made her insides bubble. Robbie got to be a nicer person, more expressive, more outgoing, friendlier; everybody noticed. Most of them thought it must be the sex. Massimo had to be rocking her world. And he was. They may have gone to their nest angry a time or two or twelve. But they never went to sleep angry. Massimo had the patience of a rock, and some of it rubbed off. Throughout the park, the coupledom of Robbie and Massimo was unquestioned. Couples had little permanence in the park, in this, theirs was unusual. The Fauves, especially, liked it. Massimo and Robbie together made them feel regular and safe, like family.

Massimo watched Robbie while she slept. She tried so hard, so hard. Her goals were so high, and she never quite reached them. He wished she could be happy.

Exo and Massimo were listening. To traffic, to kids playing over by the Meer. The construction site for a refurbished playground on 110th near Seventh Avenue was surrounded by orange plastic netting to keep people out. It made a private space for the two ghosts, gently swaying in their swings which looked like they were being pushed by the wind. It was a nice day. The whole summer had been pleasant, lots of sun, rain soft enough to stay out in.

When the trees began to lose their leaves the Hoodlums would have to do total nest disassembly. Massimo had been thinking that perhaps they could leave some of the smallest, but even they were too big for any bird anyone ever heard of. So, no, everyone's nest would have to be taken apart. (Later, in the winter, Exo built himself a nest in the pool of the Conservatory Garden. A homeless woman took it over. Almost by accident, Exo did a good deed, even though he was not supposed to interfere with life. Seeing something he did come to good was a feeling he liked.)

"It's going to rain. I can feel it in my joints." Massimo slapped his knee. He hit Exo's knee almost as hard. "People used to see me walking and think I was bopping, but I was limping. They'd look at me and think that I was cool. The truth is I was hurting." He laughed.

"How it looks ain't necessarily how it is."

"That's for sure."

Robbie liked to practice her martial arts in the promontory above The Pond. The Pond attracted bird watchers, whose patience and excitement always pleased her. Sometimes Ivan would join and they would workout together their moves a call and response of meditative self protection. But Ivan or no, Robbie kept the practice, finishing it in time to trail a living or two. It would be so easy to give up following the violinist who entered at Grand Army Plaza, met a piccolo player by the Chess and Checkers House and talked union business past Tavern on the Green and instead stay in the nest with Massimo. But what would a man with a mission like Massimo think of a woman who hadn't her own interests? Wouldn't he find that stifling?

Robbie's mind wandered; it often did these days. She brought her focus back to her posture. To keeping her fingers relaxed, not tense. To noticing her breath.

Could that be Cynthia Cox? Robbie was almost positive it was. Walking with a man below Wollman Rink . . .Cynthia? Yes! If, without any complicity from Robbie, Cynthia could see Robbie, then Robbie was on her way home. Was it possible Cynthia might be someone who might love Robbie unconditionally? Robbie had taken Cynthia for drinks and dessert that last night alive. She'd been the darn leader of the Kiss Cynthia's Ass Brigade, extending what must have been one of the happiest days of Cynthia's life. That had to count for something, didn't it? Unconditional love was built of such moments as those, no?

Wait a minute. To work, the unconditional love had to be mutual. Could Robbie honestly say that she loved Cynthia unconditionally? That she loved Cynthia at all? Robbie reasoned with herself, ambivalent. She didn't really know Cynthia well enough. She did respect how supportive Cynthia was of younger writers. And her sense of style. Today her shiny black and white leopard-spotted rain slicker and matching wide-brimmed hat were making a strong statement. And the two of them had been friends. Kind of. "What's friendship?" an art director friend once asked, and then answered his own question. "Anything over ten years."

"See me! See me!" Robbie's heart thumped as she raced to Cynthia. She would make a better go at her life this time. This time she would take the trips, build the houses, have the fun, be the first on the dance floor when she felt like dancing. She was going to be all Robbie, all the way live, all the time. She was going to come out from behind the curtain of convention. See me. Love me. Take me out of here. Robbie swooped under the umbrella.

"...Roberta Williams." Cynthia said. Robbie panicked. If she'd made herself known, it was entirely unintentional. Please, God, don't punish me. I didn't mean it. It was an accident. I don't even know how to make myself visible.

Or could it be that Cynthia did love her? Wouldn't that be wild? She'd always been nice to Cynthia; giving her leads on jobs that Robbie was too busy to handle, recommending her for writing assignments.

"Robbie Williams was supposed to get the award I got last year. I said so when they gave me the award. And then she was so nice about the afterparty, and then she was dead." Cynthia wasn't talking to Robbie, she was talking about her. Alive, Robbie hated the thought that someone might be talking about her. As a wraith, she found it deeply satisfying.

"...so talented. I wish I'd written *Warp Boy*," Cynthia was saying. "Sometimes I read a little of it, you know the part where his mother sends him away to his father's house? I read that and I cry. It's so painful."

And who is this that Cynthia is walking with, with whom she's running her mouth nonstop? Jason Du Chevaux. What is he doing with her? Jason was Robbie's white publishing daddy, not Cynthia's. Robbie was the one Jason took to lunch at Café des Artistes. She remembered distinctly his confiding that Cynthia didn't have a tenth of Robbie's talent, or beauty, or magnetism. Jason had had a little thing for Robbie once; it wasn't love. Jason and Robbie had engaged in some highly charged petting once upon a summer afternoon when most of his office had left early for the weekend. Once, in a limo, she'd crawled into Jason's lap and chewed his bottom lip. Fun and until now, nearly forgotten. What she remembered was that Jason was always scheming to get Cynthia fobbed off to another editor. And here he was, walking in the rain with her. "He always took cars with me." Robbie sniffed. A flush of embarrassment hit her like a wave. Unconditional love, indeed.

"She was a very controlled artist. Elegant. One always knew she was deciding what to share and what to hold back. Weighing how much would make the point, and then, no more. There was tension in every sentence." Robbie heard him saying.

"That's beautiful," Cynthia said.

"It is, isn't it? I like it myself," the man answered. He pushed his wire rims up on his nose.

"You should put it in your foreword on the next printing."

"Oh, God, no." Jason laughed.

"Who did you ask to accept for her?" Accept for who? For what? "It's been a long time since a person of color has been awarded the Century."

The Century? That beat the Bontemps. Way more prestigious. Robbie matched their gait, her head under the bold umbrella so as not to miss a word.

"Interesting question." Jason mused. Musing was one of his more successful poses. "I thought I'd ask her husband, but given the subject matter and her largely black audience, I don't know. I was thinking, as her publisher I could do it. But then, we've got the same problem as the husband. Cookie would be perfect, but she left the fold. And then there's . . ." he trailed.

"Who?" Cynthia said.

"How about you? You'd be just the one. You knew her..."

"Yes. We were very close."

Get out! Cynthia Cox was a creepy writer who spent all her time calling people and making lunch dates. Don't you dare let her accept my award. She got it last time. And what a rich cosmic joke if she picked one up for Robbie this time. Robbie snuggled into the humor of that. Robbie mentally shook her fist at God. "They say you have a sense of humor. I get that. A sense of humor is a very attractive quality. I can't imagine spending my life with anyone who didn't have a sense of humor. But do I always have to be the punch line?" She was sure God could see that she was in on the joke.

Winter

In winter nights the park is silent. Taxis roll through without stopping, the traffic lights on the park drive are timed to award moderate cruising. Children in the back seats of the family sedan believe their father's explanation. "I told them we were coming," as red light after red light turns green immediately upon their car's arrival. Winter, in the dark, wraiths have the park mostly to themselves. An occasional runner, rarer and rarer. Bums wandering as far from their minds as they can get found their way to other places. Cozy times.

Robbie's first blizzard was a wondrous thing. Ivan and Rodrigo and The Duchess and Massimo and Robbie were each on a branch in a maple near the pockmarked Cleopatra's Needle. Each wraith on the bow of her own strong boat. The storm advanced from the west, a thick cloud of unique white colors screaming like a herd of fierce American albinos. The wraiths could feel the storm's advance, coming like a roller coaster's up, up, up chugging. The wind was playful but too big, hiding, then blasting through, sometimes behind, sometimes to the side, sometimes right in your face. They sat in their tree with idiot grins surrounded by a thickening bright lively fog in a disappearing park. After a time there was no Met, no road, no field, only the white and the bright, and the sounds of each other's voices. "Whee!" "Wow."

A slow, low, long wow. Maybe Ivan said it. Or Robbie. Or Massimo. In college once, Robbie'd gone on a ski weekend with a freshman friend. Very wealthy. Town in Connecticut named after her forefathers. Thick blond hair. Strong bodied, tall. Mo. Her mother had gone to architecture school. The ski house was the only thing she'd ever built. Big glass walls. Small, neat bedrooms. Robbie brought her boyfriend from Harlem. (She'd gone out with the oddest guys. He was the first man she slept with, at nineteen, a man who was already twenty-six and would leave her, pregnant, to go on vacation with his old girlfriend. But that was months after the ski house trip.) They'd arrived at the ski house late in the night, in furious snow. Everyone in the house, Robbie, Mo, Page and the boyfriend, what was his name? shared a joint and sat with their feet up in the deep window seats and watched the snow dance to Thus Spake Zarathustra. Amazing how the snow turned directions, swirling in large loopy circles in time to the ponderous music. Sitting in her dormant tree, in her envelope of glistening white, Robbie wondered what those rich white people thought of her and hoped she was as exotic a blend to them as they were to her. In retrospect she thinks she must have been very beautiful. And so thin. "There's not much to you," a later lover had said to her, thus making for himself a place in her memory forever. He had a name she didn't have to search for: Sam. Our minds are lovely in the way they take care of us. Memories that hurt sharply we eventually forget. We must let go or bleed.

The snowstorm was a highlight of that dead of winter, the long stretch of January that plodded into February's tired drag toward March. The few holidays were short and cold-spirited, extra days of profit making for the merchants. The city around the park was swallowed.

But however dismal the short sun, the low hanging moisture, the stingy snows that may have made the city around it feel colorless and wan, Central Park wore gray well. It showed off her good bones, her beauty bare and serene, clean as geometry. For the livings, it was a cold winter. Homeless people crowded places the wraiths had considered their own. The banks under the Bow Bridge, below the eaves of Belvedere Castle, snuggled close to each other in the tunnel to Bethesda Fountain, these were places that wraiths found warmth. It was so obvious but Robbie never encountered anyone else there that she hadn't told about it: The mound on the hill at Compost Road. Steam comes off it; you can see that it's warm in there. Never before had there been livings in the fountains in the Conservatory Garden or the Carousel House. Brick walls that collected the sun's heat during the day and released it into the evening grew homeless livings like ivy.

"These people never go away," The Duchess complained. (She walked around naked and if she was cold she did not mention it. "Blue Blood doesn't bother with cold; it's heat we can't stand.") "We are returning to the sad state of affairs here during and after the War Between the States. You know, well actually, you probably don't know, squatters infested this area before there was a park. Oh, yes, Mr. Olmsted and Mr. Vaux had quite a time getting them out of here. Over a thousand people lived in hovels of filthy squalor. The smell from them was horrendous. In time, the police routed them and this once-lovely park was created.

"I don't know where they went, but I'm dismayed to see them back. Don't they know they're not welcomed here? I ask you, how can one enjoy beauty when such ugliness insists on intruding?" The Duchess pointed a smudged chin toward a man wrapped in newspapers, sleeping. When she was a living, Robbie hadn't liked to disagree. It occurred to her that The Duchess was very like a friend Robbie had endured who'd insisted on instructing Robbie on things Robbie already knew. The difference between Monet and Manet. How to roast fennel. The best way to negotiate a U-turn. No matter how often Robbie said, "I know. I know. I know," the friend continued. Why hadn't Robbie ever said, "Stop. I know as much as you. More." Why? Because she was too polite?

"Actually, Duchess, there might have been squalor, but there was a large, stable, prosperous old Black community here, too. They had two and three-story homes, churches, a school, a graveyard. It was called Seneca Village. Surely you knew of it?"

"Yes, you're right."

"So why do you pretend they had no rights to their homes? In Seneca the people paid for their land and built homes just like your father did."

"There were squatters. Filthy Irish. Not Black people like you. Your people were nice people who knew their place."

And had it taken from them. "I see I gave you more credit than you deserve."

"Well, aren't you full of vinegar today!"

When that winter pulled to a close Dear Old Dishwater sported a new coat. It was plaid and uglier, Ivan swore, than any she'd had before. "Doesn't do a thing for her," he said. She looked dumpier than ever, bundled against the cold. Ivan was angry, but Robbie, having Massimo, felt sorry for Dear Old Dishwater and wished Dishwater would live her life.

Spring

A family, Haitian from the looks of the father with his high-boned face and handsome posture, the two little daughters and the pregnant mother, climbed to the summit of the Great Hill. Mother was in a modest suit of navy blue with a small blue velvet hat with a short veil that covered her face to her nose. Robbie thought of advice from one of the Gigi stories, to never ask a woman why she is wearing a veil. The hat gave the woman a sober, retro look. Her girls, however, were an exuberance of color. Their dresses were brazen as flowers. One was daffodil yellow, chrysanthemum yellow, sunflower yellow, flouncing and bouncing in the waves and waves of ruffles of her bodice and skirt. The littler girl wore a rose pink dress, a peony dress, fat with layers of tulle. The satin sash had come undone and trailed behind her. Mother retied the bow. Dad, in a dark suit, sleeves a mite short, took pictures. Mother and Dad exchanged places, and Mother took pictures, the girls at the left and the right of their parents, smiling, making funny faces, squirming. Flash.

The view over Central Park West from The Great Hill was one of The Duchess' favorites. Robbie lingered there with her.

Robbie said, "My mother made our good clothes. She sewed us classic things from Vogue patterns. Plaid

Bermuda shorts, empire waisted dresses in tiny floral prints. Blouses in white cotton pique with Peter Pan collars. She never made us anything showy or trendy, no matter how pitifully we begged." Robbie talked easily with The Duchess. She was, as Ivan said, a horrible racist, clinging to passé attitudes but she was intelligent and quick and Robbie felt the racism was something she'd outgrow. The Duchess had been in the park 100 years or more, she'd seen things, she'd seen things change. "Easter was my mother's masterpiece. One year she made me a spring coat in lightweight pale lavender wool with princess seams and a gathered panel in the back. The dress was pale green, also with princess seams, in cotton velveteen. It had a large sailor collar, which Aunt Birdie crocheted in the same faint purple as the coat."

"Negroes are very particular about their children's clothes, I've noticed."

Why bother? Robbie said, "My mother took a picture of us, me, my sister and my brother. He's the youngest. It was taken after church one Sunday. We were standing in front of our garage. It had old-fashioned doors like a barn's that met in the middle and opened by hand. My brother wore a jacket that was no longer than his navy shorts. He was so cute, his face squinting into the sun. We were all squinting. It wasn't a very good picture of any one of us. My sister was chubby then, and I, an asthmatic, had my shoulders hunched up around my ears to help myself breathe. Still, we looked well loved, and as adults we loved the pictures. It was perfect of us at the time. I should have made copies for my sister and brother. I wonder who has that photograph now?"

Robbie hadn't taken any pictures of Paloma's Easter. That first Easter they hadn't even gone to church, but Robbie bought a special outfit for Paloma – Robbie sat down hard on that memory. There. Shut tight. Quiet. Breathe. Breathe. Robbie lowered her shoulders and breathed like she did before her asthma morphed into eczema.

The Duchess sat quietly, thinking perhaps, of her Easters. The dressing up, the visiting after church. The special Sunday dinner. The Haitian family finished up the film. Love, pride, color, youth, modesty – they would all show in the prints. And maybe the little girls would like the pictures when they grew up. Or maybe the family would move, or do a drastic spring cleaning some year and the pictures would be tossed. Either way, pictures are only grace notes, not melody.

Summer

To Massimo, watching the livings was like watching sports on television was to Robbie: having it on didn't bother him, but it was nothing he'd seek out on his own. Massimo wasn't adverse to hearing some gossip and, for fun, adding his own speculations, but he wouldn't make a plan of wandering the park to spy on livings. In his worldview, the livings were fiction, and he was a non-fiction kind of guy. The Fauves were his reality now. Them, Robbie and the ones who afterlifed in the park.

He was philosophical about it. After all, aren't we all stuck within our places, large or small? Once you accept that you're stuck inside of somewhere, that how you see the world is based on the position from which you see it, as a rich man or a pauper, a beauty or a beast, as a man or a woman, or as a person growing out of childhood, once you recognize that you see the world from where you are, the size of the space matters little. Massimo liked to have an effect on his space. He was his world's lover, husbanding its strengths, exalting its potentials, cajoling it into improvement, relishing its gifts. The livings were not his concern. So when Ivan and Robbie took up following their livings that summer, Massimo didn't travel with them.

It was a scalding day under a hard blue sky unsoftened by clouds. Far too hot to sunbathe on the roof over the American Wing. It was even uncomfortable on the jetty that crosses the Reservoir, although there were wraiths lounging on the rocks. Ivan and Robbie glinded about to create their own breeze. Along the Turtle Pond, down past the statue of the jaguar about to pounce where Rodrigo liked to laugh at the passers-by it startled. Up toward the museum.

"I saw a girl get killed here," Ivan said. "It was horrible. He meant to kill her. She knew it and she wasn't going to let it happen. He was so much bigger than she was. I don't know why I stayed, really. Cortez and I, he ascended some time ago now, were in a tree, cuddling, watching the traffic peter out. They say the city never sleeps, but it does. 'Round about twelve-thirty, the sidewalks roll up in Manhattan. Other places stay open much later. Madrid, of course. Berlin. Even a backwater like New Orleans has more nightlife than Gotham.

"The girl and the hulk were alone. Nobody but us chickens in the park that late at night.

"I haven't told you about Cortez, have I? Beautiful, dark eyes. Eyelashes out to here. Macho in a big way when he died, gay basher, all that stuff. Then, liberated from life, he was free to be himself, loving, open, gentle. When I get to Heaven, I'm looking for him."

Ivan waited, remembering. "The guy was laughing. He had her undies wrapped around her neck, and he was laughing. Calling her a Jew bitch. She fought for her life and he was laughing. Better I think of something else."

But he couldn't stop. "Cortez and I kept watch. A cyclist, not one of our regular soaps, found her. The big guy hung around. I saw him sitting on the wall, watching.

"Do you think in Heaven you get a fresh mind? Like you keep your personality, but any bad memories get scrubbed out? Washed pure as snow? What do you think?"

Robbie and Ivan passed by the tennis courts going uptown and downtown past the people lined up for outdoor theatre tickets. They saw no one good for gossiping or speculating about. None of their regulars was out to entertain them. No roller skaters on the blacktop in front of the band shell. No idlers under the wisteria by the lake, nobody sneaking beer on the Great Lawn. It was a hard, mean hot, dry and lifeless. Dust settled on Robbie and Ivan's skin.

"We can check out the fountain," Ivan suggested. There was a chance that in heat like this no one would be there and they could splash. Even a wraith can dream.

It struck Robbie, as it had often, how handsome Ivan was. When everyone is kind to you, as they must have been to Ivan, it's easy to be friendly. Robbie thought that she'd be friendly, too, if she'd spent her life behind Ivan's face, within his glowing, unblemished skin. He had all the luck. She felt a traitor; Ivan's friendliness was easy and comfortable, and the truth was, she herself had been told she was beautiful often enough to suspect that she'd lived with the benefits of pretty. And was she friendly? She was trying.

All she knew about Ivan was what he told her, and what she saw. She knew that he was funny and fun and full of himself and strong. Not everything that came through his mouth accurately represented him; Robbie understood this. Like her, he'd go for the laugh. He was more open with her than she with him, she suspected.

Again she was ashamed. What was wrong with her? Ivan had never been anything but nice to her. Even after he introduced her to The Duchess and whatever financial gain was gotten, he searched her out and showed her things, taught her what he thought she needed to know. Basic things like how to stop when glinding, how to avoid bumping into livings, where to rinse off. Now she was teaching martial arts to the Hoodlums, which amused Ivan to no end, and surprised Massimo. Ivan always had time for her. Deep down, she wondered why. He sat at the cool kids table, and she didn't.

There was someone at the fountain. Too bad. They couldn't go in if there was a living there. It was too easy to notice wraiths when they stood in water; water outlined them. Ivan yanked Robbie's hand. "It's him! It's him! Bartalemeo Mio." Standing close to the spraying pedestal was a young man. His own outline was clear in the sun-filled water and a rainbow of droplets shone along the sharp hump of his deltoids and down the long slope of his biceps. His waist was narrow. Languid drops lingered down his fine, long legs, his round, hard calves. Water racing down slowed to caress his feet "Be still, my heart," Ivan said, but he could not suppress himself. A spurt of ejaculate shot through the air.

"Are you always this enthused when a favorite show comes back on the air?" Robbie inquired.

Ivan babbled, laughing, hugging himself, delighted. "Do you know I followed his mother for days to discover where he was? This was back when he was, what? Twelve? Thirteen? Boarding school. For four years he was gone. Then another four for college. He has never, ever been out of my mind. Ha. Although I have been out of my mind for him...Look how he's grown." Ivan slid his tongue along his upper lip.

Looking at Bartalemeo Mio made you wish you had one. He was tall and sturdy, a riot of juicy color: pale skin so smooth it looked like it might ripple if touched, orange bright hair, tight to his head, squirming wildly on his crown. A cleft centered in his square chin, lashes thick as a dust storm fringed his clear blue eyes. His pupils were alarmingly dark. "I feel he's staring at me," Ivan said. It seemed so to Robbie also, although she knew the young man couldn't see them.

Another festive "Orchestra Under the Stars" night. The mayor, who looked like he was separated at birth from Frank Perdue, stomped between picnic blankets waving both hands beside his shoulders exclaiming, "Hey! It's me!" In answer there was mostly silence spiced with a few boos. "Stick your foot in your mouth," a deep voice yelled. A good-looking male tennis star wandered amid the blankets, trailed by a whispered buzz. Those who arrived early had staked out areas for friends who came after work. They covered their blankets with baskets of food and candlesticks and tethered high-flying helium balloons and flags and banners to ID their spaces. The crowd waxed. Couples searched for the right balloons and banners. Police patrol with Park Rangers in Mounties' hats. With good humor they ordered people to stay out of the fire lanes.

New York City is a zoo. A collection of all the world's variation, pure, blended, mutated. Hummingbird men, their legs thin, their lips ceaselessly flittering on phones. Palomino runners, golden in reflections from a million windowpanes, limbs syncopated, members joining and leaving the herd. Huff. Huff. Huff. Four Black women, their narrow heads erect, their hair sleek and glossy as feathers, stalk, long legged, high and hard butted, across the grassland. Where they are from, does the snow fall pink? Does it glitter instead of rain?

Above the crowd in a tree just to the west of the orchestra Robbie and Massimo had a good view of almost everything. They'd come early and watched the playing fields fill with young women in their New York black work dresses carrying a United Nations of take-out, salmon mousse, pita bread, fried okra with hot sauce, fresh fried donuts, fresh-fried catfish sandwiches and lobster salad from Zabar's. Girls with potato salad and red wine and meatball heroes and hummus and stuffed grape leaves and bottled water met the young men who'd spent their afternoons tossing Frisbees. By the time the dignitaries made their brief speeches and briefer introductions, the sun was dropping. The conductor ambled onstage, dark, bald and hugely fat. With no ado Schubert's Symphony #8 in B minor began.

"Wake me up when the fireworks start," Massimo said.

"Don't you dare sleep," Ivan said, holding his arm up for Massimo to pull him into the branches. Massimo reached down and Ivan leapt and settled in on the branch below Robbie and Massimo. If you saw the tree trembling you would have thought it was the wind. "Listening to the music is the price we must pay for the fireworks." Two minutes into the music Ivan's eyes closed. Massimo snuggled his head into Robbie's lap and closed his eyes. Robbie's eyes stayed open, her ears, even her lips were open to suck in every note until the applause exploded. During the Firebird the sky faded soft pink and quiet blue. Picnicking groups freed their balloons, great grape bunch shapes of color drifted into the sky. Talkers got shushed. At the final selection, the crowd tried to concentrate, tried to be polite and pay attention, but the haunting, melodic Tchaikovsky couldn't capture the crowd's mind. Fireworks were due. The crowd expected them at every drum roll, at every crescendo. At every crash, heads turned skyward for fireworks. The music ended with nothing.

The fireworks burst. Louder than any music, raining color throughout the sky, dribbling silver and gold and disappearing blue. As always with fireworks, there weren't enough. The air filled with gray smoke. The fields emptied. An orderly crowd had gotten what it came for.

"Wrap your memories carefully," Ivan whispered. The way the moon rose over the music. Gold sparkles dripping against a midnight blue sky. These were the things Robbie would save. In the coming cold she would unwrap them and share them with Massimo. Remember how big and low the moon was? How it outlined the skyline? Remember you closed your eyes and I stroked your eyelids with my fingertips? Remember?

"Look!" Ivan pointed to a couple still on their blanket among the standing groups busy collecting their emptied wine bottles, their leftover plates. Between blankets being shaken free of dead leaves and dry grass was the sliver of a view of a woman, her head resting deep against a t-shirted masculine chest, her eyes closed, tendrils of hair washing back from her restful face. A man's hand caressed that head. Dear Old Dishwater, displayed like a jewel in the velvet of her contentment.

The man stood and extended a hand to pull her up. She rose on her own, awkwardly. He picked up a camera and said something to her. She shook her head no. He put his palms together in a prayer gesture. Please? Dear Old Dishwater posed. She was wearing loose pants with an elastic waist. The color was toreador bright red and they were toreador length showing off her muscular calves. She had on a peasant blouse with a gathered yoke, the kind that can stretch to wear down past the shoulders. She wore it pushed down that way and embroidered Mexican figures danced across her plump breasts. Her hair had grown and she wore it back in a low ponytail, curls escaping near her face. The man was thin and sharp featured; he looked like a second string player in a 40's movie, "half smart." He'd be the guy with the gun and the itchy fingers that the hero would disable with his fist. A worry line snaked across his forehead.

"She looks so happy," Robbie breathed.

"See how beautiful she is in love?" Ivan said. Her toes were free, nakedness so sad Robbie resisted voicing that the man wasn't good enough for their girl. With her coat gone, her personal stereo gone, her toes unprotected in the air and dust, it didn't seem like Dishwater was shielded by her lover's hairy arms; those arms were the mouth of a hole into which Dear Old Dishwater was sinking. But she sank happily. The field was empty before the couple sighed and her young man tucked their threadbare blanket under his arm and the two slipped silently away from the Great Lawn.

"He looks like he's married to somebody else." Ivan said. When Robbie had been in elementary school she'd had a babysitter who watched soaps. When Robbie got home Miss Emily was deep in the couch watching her "stories," scolding the women on the TV screen for listening to the lies of the men, disgusted with the men for falling for the demon women, talking to them as if they could hear her advice. Robbie felt for Ivan, but he was no more able to affect Dishwater's story than Miss Emily was able to change the course of *The Days of Our Lives*.

Winter Again

When she had been alive Halloween had been Robbie's favorite holiday. The children in costumes wandering the streets, trailing their parents. She still watched the jack o'lanterns float on the Meer. But now, New Year's Eve was Robbie's favorite night. Central Park's New Year's is the brightest of this brightest of nights, a group fresh start, an opportunity in unison to get it right this time. Fireworks blow simultaneously at 96th, 86th, and 66th Streets. The crowd sparkles. Tavern on the Green is done up in lights, millions of tiny lights wrapped around the trees, their trunks and branches all the way to the tips and ornamented with large glass balls veined with gold, Venetian in their beauty. Strangers wish each other a Happy New Year. Champagne bottles are passed from lips to lips. Baby-faced policemen wish a "Happy New Year!" to citizens.

It's glorious.

Excitement's light shone in Robbie's, Massimo's and Ivan's faces. They mingled between the clusters of livings. Rodrigo, ever dirtier and more disreputable-looking, had spun by, on the trail of a troupe of wandering drummers who attracted dancers wherever they stopped and spread their rhythms. Robbie had been tempted to follow with him. She'd enjoyed these drummers many Sunday afternoons at Bethesda

Fountain. Rodrigo said their drumming called down spirits and tonight he had an appointment to communicate with them. Could be, but Rodrigo was such a liar. Robbie waved her goodbye greetings. "Tell them I said hello." The Duchess pleaded tiredness a half-hour before when the crowd was just beginning to assemble. Massimo had lifted her up by her armpits and kissed her for the New Year and The Duchess had permitted it.

"Next year we'll see each other in Heaven!" Robbie hung between Massimo and Ivan, her arms around their shoulders. It could happen. All she had to do was...what?

"And leave here? Don't be absurd," Ivan said.

Yes, and why not? They were in a place where people came to play, to be happy, a place of recreation and fantasy. Maybe there was no Heaven other than understanding that this was lovely enough. For sure, her lover was an angel. Suspecting his boys had planned something for him, Massimo hadn't wanted to come downtown. He'd come to please Robbie, who'd refused to stay uptown. The living Robbie would have stayed with her boyfriend even if it meant giving up something she wanted to do more. She was working on it, and it seemed significant to her, on the eve of a New Year to break old habits and forge new ways. Such is the power of the slide of one year into the unbroken promise of a new one. And here Massimo was, unresentful, having, if anything, a better time than she.

A man played rock flute across the road from Tavern on the Green and two girls freer than birds danced with each other to his music. Mink coats abounded. A huff of runners, many in costumes, awaited the starting gun for the Roadrunners Club Midnight Run, jouncing under a balloon arch.

"Happy New Year!" Ivan yelled above the merry din. His shapely chest swelled. Massimo covered Robbie's face and neck with kisses. Ivan ran kisses from hands up to her shoulders. "Happy New Year. Happy New Year!" Robbie shouted to the world. The start gun fired and a rush of hardcore runner crazies in ape heads, mixed with a corps of runners in tights and tutus, some with down vests over their ensembles, took off.

Two women stand in the dreary left-behind, a yellow blond and a platinum, both holding armloads of clothing that clearly belong to running boyfriends.

"Last year I was at the St. Regis," the yellow blond said. "At midnight I was dancing with Richard. Balloons cascaded from the ceiling, we kissed and sipped champagne." She paused. Smoke from fireworks was floating to the grass. She stepped from left to right, from right to left in her heels. She adjusted the bundle of clothes in her arms. The suit jacket and the down jacket slipped on their hangers. Their sleeves grazed the damp pavement. Small groups passed round the two blonds, on to whatever was next. "You know what I'm doing tomorrow?" the yellow blond asked. A reveler tossed a bottle towards a nearby trash can and missed.

The platinum nodded. "Calling Richard."

It's better to be a runner than the girlfriend of a runner, Robbie thought.

"Let's run with them," Massimo said.

"Brilliant," Robbie breathed. Death had taken none of Massimo's physical spirit away from him. What he missed most was the immediate, present and very satisfying exertion he felt from weightlifting. There was nothing to replace it in afterlife. But a race, now that got him going. And while he spun thoughts of organizing an Olympics for his boys, he took off. Of course, running with livings was no challenge at all and challenge was what he wanted. Robbie and Ivan hung back at the front of the pack, but Massimo's joy was in a burst of effort. "I'll see you at the finish line." His grin was all excitement and perfect teeth.

Fireworks colors popped and glittered above, from outside the park now, from rooftops uptown. The air was thick with the sizzle and crack of rockets, strong footfalls and the sporadic singing of revelers. And bagpipes. The footfalls were quick and tight at the start; they hit a rhythm that evened out to a prayer. Above 96th Street, the breathing was louder. Dark surrounded. The joyous crowd sobered as they realized that no matter how high their spirits, the circuit around Central Park was still six miles long and much of it was uphill. Ivan and Robbie kept pace with the leads, two determined men struggling against each other, the hills, age. The prize would be bragging rights. Pity the friends of the man who won. Ivan knew them from his soaps. Ed Campbell and John Fager.

Snow floated down, light, airy, magical. It softened the parks' hard edges. Tomorrow fresh debris would fall, dropped by careless jerks who would never enjoy the park after they died and scarce appreciated it, or anything, while they lived. Tonight, though, was the snow's triumph. Ivan and Robbie passed the loudspeaker car alerting people to get out of the way of the onrush of runners; this too was muffled by snow.

Robbie loved the night like this. Even with the crowd, it felt private. The snow thickened the space between beings, encapsulating in solitude and conversely, connecting more fully. Stop a moment. Isn't that Dear Old Dishwater there on the Great Hill? Between the trees in an oversized coat with a hood?

Look, she left a bundle on that broken bench. About the size of a bag of groceries.

It was dark at this end of the park, even with the snow. The figure was in the shadows, still, Robbie was almost certain it had been Dear Old Dishwater. It had walked like Dear Old Dishwater; she knew that walk. Where did she disappear to? The bundle started crying.

"Babies?" Robbie flew to the bench. Three tiny sets of fists were thumping the air; three little faces tight with fury. "They're babies!"

Paloma had never been so tiny. But her fists had been as tight, and her eyes had been as tender, and her hands had looked as if they screwed into the wrists, so short and definite and clear the line between hand and wrist had been. And the nails. Like razors. And if she scratched herself in half an hour it was healed with no sign of where the cut had been. Her lungs had been as strong. Stronger, even. Paloma had a little hat tied off at the top, she didn't look like her mother or her father, with her squashed newborn swollen beautiful face. Like the faces of these newborns.

Ivan held Robbie back. "There's nothing you can do."

"I can save them. I can carry them to a spot where someone will see them." She was thinking that on the road the runners would surely find them. A group of runners could round the curve by the compost driveway and stumble over a hump of crying babies, the runners behind bumping into them and everyone forgetting the race for the prize and racing instead across Fifth Avenue carrying the newborns to Mt. Sinai. It'd make a great New Year's story.

"Don't interfere. Or do you want to be stuck here forever? I'll tell you this: the park was once beautiful all over. Now it isn't. It only gets worse. This is the best it's going to be which isn't nearly as nice as it was, even twenty years ago. Compared to forever twenty years is the blinking of an eye. This is too tiny a place for forever. Believe me."

"I can't stay here and listen to them die."

"Then go. I'll stay."

So they stayed while the last runner pulled up the lagging rear. The hills grew whiter and rounder and more beautiful, peaceful as healthy pregnant women.

"Hey, people. What happened? I was waiting for you." Massimo bounded up the Great Hill, his voice a mixture of complaint and relief. "Que pasa?" He approached like a camp counselor, assistant athletic director, enthusiastic and eager to share. But Massimo was not an insensitive man. He entered Robbie and Ivan's silence. A small wail came faintly, still angry and hopeful. Massimo glinded to the park bench. Ivan's hand rested on Massimo's shoulder, and Massimo retreated to wait with the others.

Robbie wondered about squandering her life. She'd been blessed with so much -- talent, health, friends, a loving husband, a beautiful bundle of sweet love daughter – and accomplished so little with it. Would she squander her death, too? Would she give in to momentary impulses, and forfeit the big prize? It felt so right to save those babies. Babies. They still had a chance. Would she choose their chance over her own? Was she ready to claim their lives were more valuable than her own future? There were rules. She could choose to break them. That would be giving up. Would she tell the universe that she wasn't valuable? Wouldn't that be a slap in the face of whoever deemed life for her?

Eventually, the crying stopped. Eventually, the bundle was still. On New Year's Day only runners and a couple of cross country skiers were up early. None of them came near the top of the hill at the top of the park. It was a honey of a day. Soft Turneresque yellows down to the horizon, a silvered turquoise band shimmering on the treetops. Holding tight to Massimo's waist as they wandered the Ramble, Robbie wondered who she was that she'd let babies die to save herself.

Ivan took the bundle to The Duchess.

"Triplets," The Duchess exclaimed.

"Winken, Blinken and Nod," Ivan said. "Twenty-eight, twenty-nine, thirty."

"You can choose your jewel tomorrow," she lied.

Oddly enough, the babies grew. Irrespective of the rules prohibiting it, the three grew to be chubby, filling out their wrinkles with cuteness. Maybe because they were preemies, their growth already programmed, but cut short by in utero crowding. Maybe it was love.

Summer

Robbie was there when Gloria died. It was a nice summer night, the trees their darkest green, the moon a pale quarter, the crowd settling into the chairs lined up that evening by parkies into rows in front of the band shell. The sky was deepening to a romantic light, encouraging hand holding, or between the shy or newly met, tapping on arms with tentative fingertips. Women in sleeveless blouses wore their dates' arms around their shoulders. It was a small crowd, but mighty. A conversational buzz, the scraping of chairs against pavement, stage whispers from one couple to another as friends who did not want to sit together acknowledged each other with waves and nods.

Robbie couldn't remember a literary event where she hadn't expected herself to work the room. Lots of times she let herself down and didn't step up and meet new publishers and bookstore owners, she hung back from the patrons of the arts generally behaving as if they wouldn't be pleased to meet her. She hadn't always been "on" and quick with the witty remark, but she'd always felt she should be. Tonight, two writers were going to read from their work and all Robbie had to do was listen and enjoy. Death had its advantages.

She sat cross-legged on top of a six-foot tall speaker whose vibrations tickled her intestines. From there she had a view of the stage and the audience. Robbie made a game of matching who was in the audience to who was reading. They were mostly Black and Latino. Who said African Americans didn't read? The young man with the short Afro and the wire rims over a gentle face was there for Paula Washington. One was always surprised at how large a body of work Ms. Washington had produced, all of it excellent. Her career had been quiet, and steady; she taught at one college, then another, and turned out a well-reviewed book every four years or so. A serious, beautiful writer who respected English. In the back, a couple of lesbians drank from a brown paper bag. Probably something good; they didn't look like the Night Train type. Office clothes, good haircuts. Pre-mixed Margaritas maybe. Or Black Russians, a winter drink, but one that tasted good unchilled. Maybe they were sipping straight Jack. Robbie bet they were there for Gloria Nyabonga. An interesting woman. Rumors swarmed about her like flies. That she was a junkie. That she was a nympho. That she had enemies she didn't know she had because she cussed them out and been too drunk to remember, but not too drunk to say exactly the thing that would sting now and throb later. She was an exciting writer and a daring performer of her work, and that she would most probably be high while performing only added to the frisson. Robbie was more interested in seeing her, too.

Gloria Nyabonga hadn't read in Central Park since she'd fallen off the stage four years ago. She'd dislocated her shoulder and presented the city with her medical bill. The city had refused to pay. After that, sponsors shied away and program directors had been afraid to accept responsibility. The new program director – no one who headed the program stayed for long – was an admirer and a bit of a radical and a bully and found it ridiculous that a woman whose work was meant to be read aloud wasn't included in the roster of writers in the program, so what if she fell off the damn stage. Madame La Program Director personally lined the proscenium with sandbags three-high. It looked ugly, but ugliness was a radical statement.

Gloria was glad to be back. The fee wasn't much, but they did put you up in a nice hotel, and it was good to get to New York with someone else footing the bill. She lived across the river in Jersey City and could be home in under an hour, but Gloria liked to get hers. Later on tonight she'd go down to SOB's and shake some booty. She knew the doorman there, or used to, who'd let her in for free. And men would always buy her drinks. That was one of the many things she liked about being a woman. Women didn't have to pay if they didn't want to. Of course, she had gone into her pockets, deeply, many times for men, some of who hadn't been worth a dime. Some of them didn't even make good material for a short story. At least not an original short story.

Paula Washington was up first. She read with an innocence that belied the darkness deep in her stories. Her work was disturbing, no less because she was a pretty, non-threatening woman, someone you'd put in front of a classroom of children without a moment's worry. She read two stories, the second of which made the audience laugh in several spots. Tomorrow there'd be a slight bump in her book sales at Barnes and Noble on 83rd Street and Hue-Man up in Harlem. When she was finished and welcomed Gloria to the stage, the picture was the strong sister hugging the wild sister. Both worth interest and not at all in competition. It was Paula's kiss that energized Gloria's poem about how many women are battered every few minutes, how many raped, how many killed. Gloria's own power amped the rest of her performance. Tonight Gloria was on a Judeo-Christian rant.

"God was a terrible parent," she said. "Can you imagine sending your innocent child off to die a painful death preceded by three days of torture? Wouldn't you figure out a way to spring your child from jail? A parent who didn't do anything about that — and could — wouldn't you ask some questions? Hire a better lawyer? Something?" The crowd tittered nervously. "But no. . . Jesus even asked God, 'Please, don't make me go through with this,' and God said, 'Sorry, Kid. I love you, but it is written.' It is written? That's like telling someone what the company policy is. We all know that company policy is for the slobs that don't have any connections at all. For the people who have to go to personnel to get permission to take an extra two vacation days. Written? Well, erase it and get a rewrite." The laughs were stronger now. "This is what God does to a child He's pleased with?" Gloria made a telephone receiver with her fingers and talked into the mouthpiece. "Excuse me, Social Services? There's some child abuse happening over here you should know about.

"The only thing that saves Him from being absolutely a bad example is that we are his children, too. And he sacrificed that one for the rest of us. But what would make Him a good parent would be if He sacrificed Himself.. Isn't that what we expect from a good parent? 'I'll take your bullets?'

"I've got to tell you, God's parenting confuses the hell out of me. Not a good role model, especially considering He's supposed to be Father to us all. Maybe that's what faith is all about. Maybe the bedrock of that religion is God is different from you and me and we've got to forgive God for that. Apply different standards."

After the reading, Luke, Gloria's bodyguard, wanted her to hurry, but Gloria didn't have hurry in her after a performance. She liked to greet the people who came to praise her, to linger in the warm memory of applause while she had a toke or two.

"It's a dangerous place," Luke said. He'd waited until the small crowd around Gloria had their say, but he was all business and haste now.

"It's in the middle of the damn park. Less than a hundred yards from here there're at least a hundred rollerbladers." Gloria waved him away. She was deep into her incense. She meditated a lot. Went into herself. It was almost spooky the way she did it. It was completely as if she weren't there. Luke didn't feel good about it.

"Come on. I can't wait for your tired old ass, I got a date tonight." Luke was big shouldered and on the short side. Most of his wardrobe was designer sweatpants and color-coordinated knit shirts.

"Who'd be dumb enough to make a date with you?" She joked. "I know. Valerie."

"Val was two weeks ago. Linda."

"Linda's not so dumb."

"No, she's not." In fact, Linda was a reach for Luke. She was smart, and not delicate, like you didn't have to watch what you said around her all the time; she fought back if you flicked her with a wet towel. "So get off your high yellow behind and let's haul it out of here."

"Have fun."

"I'm not leaving you here alone."

"Go. Go."

"You're ruining my love life."

"You're ruining your own love life. I'll be fine. Go." She waved her joint in the air. Then extended it towards him, offering. He shook his head. "Go."

Robbie watched. There was no backstage at the band shell, simply a stone walled restroom. She thought the muscular guy was right. Gloria should have protection late at night in the park. Gloria was the kind of person things happened to.

Luke didn't like it, though. Gloria was right, the park wasn't deserted, and he wasn't really a bodyguard as much as a personal assistant with muscles, and he had a date with a woman who might find some interesting things to do without him if he was late. Still, he couldn't leave Miss Nyabonga in the park alone. He had to get her back to her hotel lobby at least. "Come on, let's go."

Gloria had a satchel full of stuff that she took with her, that she had him carry. Luke had explained to her more than once, like a thousand times, that she should carry her own stuff (most of it unnecessary so far as he could tell – how many broken cigarettes did a person need?) her own books, her own pens, pencils, make-up, toothbrush, diary, calendar, calcium pills, so that he could keep his mind and body totally attentive to her safety. No one had ever tried to attack anything but her feelings, and the biggest part of his job was to tell her sincerely that the other guy was an asshole. Still, how could he bodyguard with his arms full of paraphernalia? He grunted as he lifted her bag, "Do you have your laptop in here?" So when Ms. Nyabonga dropped dead of a heart attack Luke's sizeable arms were loaded down with her stuff. There was nothing Luke could have done that he wasn't doing already.

Robbie had never in her life acted straight from her desire, but when Gloria died, Robbie didn't even let

Gloria sleep. She didn't think about her own rest between dying and afterlife. Or that she met Massimo when he was waking up after he'd been stabbed. Robbie was on Gloria like white on rice; she didn't consider that she might be robbing Gloria of something she needed. Robbie was that hungry for a girlfriend. A woman who named the world the same way she did. Someone who loved words and dance and theatre. Who had corns from wearing her cute shoes too small. Here was the possibility of friendship that didn't have to be squeezed into a long lunch or a dinner every month or so. Their days would be free to spend with each other, dishing, laughing. Here was the possibility of a friendship that might fulfill a fantasy Robbie cherished as a living – spending her days doing what she liked, and her evenings with a husband who'd spent his days doing what he liked. Massimo had his boys. Ivan moped around after Bartalemeo Mio. Robbie wanted Gloria.

So Gloria was awake for the aftermath of her demise.

Despite Luke's feelings of isolation, there were a lot of good people around in the park and his shout brought help immediately. A crowd gathered at the news of a death and swelled at the rumor that it was somebody famous, and a couple of reporters came. No news cameras, though. Gloria laughed. "Story of my life, file footage. The press was always six months behind me."

Robbie followed Gloria as Gloria followed her body from pavement to stretcher to ambulance. "Bless my soul, he lifted me like I weighed nothing." Gloria eyed the medic. "I love a man who can make me feel like a woman." She eyed her dead body, bouncing in response to the medic's hands pumping between her meaty breasts. "Buy me a drink first, lover. What kind of a girl do you think I am?" She laughed. She leaned over her resting face with its Mona Lisa smile. "Look how small I look." She preened a little. The paramedic covered her body and face.

"Life keeps weight on you," Robbie said.

Luke wouldn't confess that Gloria had been smoking dope. "I don't know anything about that," he said, shifting from one foot to the other by the gurney, but pot smell was strong on her clothes.

"I don't think it had anything to do with her death," the doctor patted Luke's shoulder. Luke struggled not to cry, but his nose was running like tears. Gloria's body was slid into the ambulance and the doors slammed shut.

"You want to follow them to the perimeter?" Robbie said. "We can't leave the park, but we can go to the end. We can ride on top. I'll pull you up."

"Nah. I don't like ambulances." Gloria said. Robbie remembered that Gloria had been involved in more than her share of fist fights and gun brandishings and police being called. She knew better than most that ambulances were for hurt people. The public servants got in their cars and carts and went away. "So, tell me what's up."

While the crowd dispersed and the parkies stacked the chairs, Robbie told Gloria what Ivan had told her. "We can't eat?" Gloria said. Robbie told her no. "Do we get hungry?" No. "Do we do the dirty deed?" Robbie smiled.

The women discovered they knew some of the same livings – had even dated the same man, (both briefly) and had the same opinion about him. Gloria, had never even heard of Cynthia Cox. No writer, present company excepted, was as good as either of them. "Or as deserving," Robbie said.

Gloria hooted. "Deserving? Deserving has nothing to do with it. Who made that shit up? There're women who eat whatever they want and their stomachs are never anything but flat, and their legs go on forever, and their boobs never fall. And there are women who never eat anything they want and they have cellulite at twenty-five. Nice guys can't get the girls and the girl they end up with is a bitch. Dogs marry the twins to Mother Teresa and then cheat on them."

"Mozart had the music just come to him. He didn't work for it. Sometimes I think that in art, working for something, convincing yourself that you've earned it, is a sure way not to get it." Gloria was loud. Robbie was amazed that the livings didn't hear her. "The only way you can receive from the Universe is to recognize what you get as a gift. It's all a gift, you know. No matter how hard you work, whatever you get is a gift. Working is just our way of obscuring that. Damn. I should write that down. That was heavy. What makes it more heavy is I don't have a clue where it came from. Goes to prove my point." Gloria's sentences went on and on, ending up far away from where they started, unconnected except by the route they followed to get from A to B on their way to wherever. Only Gloria could guide you on that route and she could do it only once. "It's all ego. Remember the lilies of the field? They toil not, et cetera? You have to accept that the Creator provides, not you. You deserve according not to what you do, but what you receive. I didn't deserve a heart attack, but here I am. It's not so bad." She nudged Robbie's thigh with her knee, a touch both playful and intimate. "I've been hanging with spirits a long time. Now I'll be one. Cool."

On the days before she was buried, Gloria read to Robbie. Newspapers, advertisements bolted atop taxicabs, "Alive with Pleasure. Newport." "It's a Woman

Thing. Benson and Hedges." A book, *Das Kapital*, left behind by a sunbather in the Shakespeare Garden. Gloria read it only when no one was there to see, and put it back right where it'd been, every time someone approached.

"I'm tired. You tell me a story," Gloria said.

In the hot spotlight of Gloria's attention, Robbie said, "There was once a woman and her husband and they had a daughter. They named her Jewel, for she was more precious than gold to them. Jewel was kind and smart and beautiful. Although her parents were poor, no princess was better trained in the skills of social intercourse. They taught her good manners and proper dress, to always present herself with pride and to behave toward all people as if they were royalty, and to receive such treatment from everyone. Jewel's parents gave her the very best education they could, and with her scholarship she was able to go to the most excellent university in the country. It was there that the king's son and the poor parents' daughter met and liked each other, and respected each other and found so much about each other that was pleasing that they fell in love The king's son asked Jewel to marry him and be his bride.

"In that country it was the custom for the wife's family to pay for the wedding. The wedding of a Prince is a very big affair, with many guests to be seated and fed and made comfortable and merry. The prince's parents planned the wedding and invited the girl's parents, who the king and queen found to be proud, witty, charming - an altogether attractive couple. Imagine their surprise when the bride's parents objected. They planned to follow custom and pay for the wedding. They could not afford the extravagances the reigning couple could, hence, the wedding would be a simpler affair. The guests' coaches were parked by local farmhands dressed in their best suits, their trousers legs some a wee mite too short and others, trippingly long. Still, their manners, if rough, came from respectful hearts and although the parking lot was a field with grasses cut down, the day was beautiful and spring flowers lent their sharp colors and sweet aromas. The rented wooden chairs were set up in the farmer's back yard where the young groom waited with his father, the king, and the bishop under a wide flowering canopy with the smell of grapes intoxicating the golden air. The whole afternoon had the attitude of a day off from school without adult supervision and guests were giddy with nature. When the farmer walked his daughter down the aisle, all could see that the farmer and the farmer's wife knew: that their treasure was equal to all the king's.

"The cake, fit for a king, was a gift of the king and queen. The bride's father, whose uncle was vintner of some reputation, provided the wine. Everyone fell in love a little that day, which is what happens at good weddings."

"Nice story."

"I made it up for my daughter when I was pregnant."

"How old was she?"

"Fifteen months."

Massimo knew about Gloria. Robbie talked about Gloria, and not everything she said was flattering. She told Massimo things about Gloria that were attractive, but presented in a way that he could feel between the lines. And when he questioned her, "But don't you think she went too far when she..." Robbie would laugh and hit his arm and tell him not to be so critical. Massimo left it alone. He'd never been one for hanging out with women; there were men, fully heterosexual, who enjoyed being one of the girls from time to time. They were the men from whom a woman could comfortably ask for a man's opinion and get it. A girl could call a guy like that in the middle of the night when she was feeling low. A guy like that could have women friends without giving his wife reason for anything other than gratitude to the Almighty. Massimo wasn't a guy like that. He also heard about Gloria from the wraiths who'd bedded her. She embraced her role of nearly live fresh newbie with legendary vigor.

Gloria's funeral was at St. John the Divine. Mourners crowded the cathedral. There were as many laughs as tears, a plenitude of both. Robbie and Gloria learned this as a group of Gloria's friends made its way downtown through the park after the service. They entered from Frederick Douglass Circle, giggly, tipsy and outright drunk. Robbie and Gloria flitted from tree to tree up Harlem Hill, watching the parade of people who loved Gloria. If Gloria was your friend no one could do you wrong without feeling her fierceness. She was the hard shell for her tender friends.

Gloria was having great fun making fun of her friends as they passed beneath her. "Look at Cyrus wearing a white suit, trying to look like Geoffrey Holder," she scoffed. "He needs to give it up and lose some weight."

Cyrus himself was scolding Thelma, who refused to acknowledge his flagrant homosexuality. "Don't be hanging on me, Thelma, unless you want to be sitting down on the street. I can hardly keep myself upright." And Roger, in a wheelchair. That was new. Suzette and Suzanne, the chic and the slutty, both actually very nice girls, but twins fighting their identicalness with opposing styles. Dark Chanel suit with pearls and pins, black tube top with Capri pants under a bolero jacket, also black, but wrinkled. They'd been crying. And there was Ramon with his suave self, sniffing after Suzette. Dog. As if he didn't have a new baby at home.

Robbie seriously considered not telling Gloria about being able to escape back to life. After all, it might not even be true. And what if Robbie told it to Gloria wrong? Robbie didn't really know many details, how it all worked. Would the livings automatically see a wraith they felt unconditional love for without the wraith making any moves of her own? Or did a wraith have to present herself? And if a wraith showed herself and the unconditional love wasn't there, would Heaven be forbidden to that wraith forever?

And here's the truth: Robbie didn't want Gloria to go.

But how could Robbie not tell Gloria about getting out? If there would ever be a chance for it, this was it. Just maybe Gloria could this very day be drinking wine, smoking dope, writing a new poem for publication or private pleasure. Her chance was passing beneath her feet and Robbie had to tell her.

"There's this story that if a living who feels unconditional love for you finds you in the park, they can take you out a living. Unconditional love brings you back to life." Robbie said.

"Oh, yeah?"

"I heard a story where that happened. It happened to one of the Fauves. His name was Tre and one day he was playing with his friend Phillip, and his dog named Gristle, who was alive, came upon him in the park, slobbered on him like he was alive, and they walked out of the park together, onto Central Park West.

"If you position yourself down there among your people, you can probably get out of here."

"I don't want to." Gloria stared down from her branch at her pageant of handsome people in black. Gloria wanted to see her mommy and daddy, but they wouldn't be walking through the park. She wished for them, for one last hug, a long, send-off hug in which their love and their confidence in their daughter and the job they'd done with her would be clear in every muscle, in the way they held her to their breasts and in the way they held her away. "Act pretty," they'd say. She already had that hug. Her parents had given it to her many times. Many times and each time they could not have meant it more or communicated their love more surely. Perhaps they were already in a car on their way to LaGuardia for a flight back to West Palm Beach. "My life was good. I want to see what's next."

Robbie was with Gloria when Gloria's body was laid to rest and gravity gave her up. Robbie tried to cast herself in the nursemaid role, but Gloria wasn't having it. Gloria was evil personified during her temperature loss. She ate dirt, kicked at wraiths. She cried into Robbie's lap, then tried to bite Robbie's navel off. Robbie hung in there like Ivan had for her; it was like being the husband at his child's delivery – cursed out, slapped, and when it's over, nobody notices you.

Two black women, close in age with similar interests, their friendship made all the sense in the world. But underneath they were not the same at all. Gloria was all bright colors and exuberance and rowdy noise. Robbie was elegance and reserve and considerations. Gloria put out. Robbie holds back. Robbie thought Gloria's openness was unsafe and pampered. Gloria didn't understand why Robbie wasn't the same way. Robbie wanted to change, Gloria was happy with the way she was.

Even when she was alive Robbie had never felt jealousy for Gloria. It would have been like a shepherdess being jealous of Athena, the favorite daughter of the king of the gods. It wasn't that Gloria's writing was so wonderful, it was her talent for developing an audience. Gloria had passed from the public's respect to the public's ownership. Not for Gloria Nyabonga confinement to the arts pages. She was news on Entertainment Tonight. Big and "yaller" in the gossip page photos she was usually taller than her men were. Her 5'11" height, her hair (braids with blond and blue extensions) and her sailor's mouth gave her a drag queen's presence. In a group of transvestite divas, she did not stand out as the most feminine. When she died, at forty-seven, she was still enjoying one-night stands with weight-lifting bouncers.

Gloria had always felt free to step out there; she always had somewhere comfortable to fall. If she lost her mind, or couldn't pay her rent, or needed somewhere to go between adventures, she could always crash in her old room in her parents' house with en suite and cleaning lady Tuesdays and Fridays. Gloria's parents loved her; even her mother's "Smells like Gloria's back," was sighed with affection.

Gloria played hairdresser with Robbie's hair, which she thought Robbie should do something with. She collected leaves with which to decorate Robbie's waist. "If I had a waist like yours, I'd string bells around it." Even without a waist like Robbie's, Gloria wore a string settled around her hips with three bells on it. She wore it to celebrate her hips, which were wide, and which Gloria had forced herself to love. Loving her hips had given birth to a whole body of loving. "I am never ashamed of myself. Never."

The Duchess didn't care for Gloria. And why should she? Gloria sucked up all the attention. No matter how outrageous The Duchess was, Gloria was more so. No matter how much attention The Duchess demanded, Gloria was paid more. The Duchess stomped her perfect little dirty feet, Gloria laughed and tossed her fake hair. Ivan enjoyed the tension between them. Ivan liked Gloria quite a lot. She could be as sexy dirty as he was and just as open about her enjoyment of smut. She could trade him sex story for sex story, no euphemisms allowed. The Duchess refused to remain in the presence of that kind of talk. It wasn't suitable for the children. What purpose those innocents had to accomplish before Heaven no one knew, but they were adorable.

Most days Gloria gravitated to the Sheep Meadow because of the dope smoke in the air. "I'd still like a shot of bourbon." Gloria's appetites maintained themselves like desert plants, alive without nourishment. "Hah! I never sat down to write without a drink, or a joint, or both, and a good book, or maybe a trashy one, and at least one magazine. If I deprived myself while I was writing, my writing came out deprived. Deprivation in, deprivation out. I was never a monk."

"But sometimes I felt like I had to get high to know what you were saying."

"Why didn't you?" Gloria hovered beside a group of young men in yellow t-shirts, probably from a school running club. "Breathe deep and hold your breath," she said to Robbie. "Don't tell me you never smoked herb."

"I smoked herb," Robbie dutifully said, holding her breath while she talked.

"What's the problem, then? You afraid you'll give up Heaven if you get high? God's not going to punish you for having a good time. Listen to me," Gloria let go of smoke and gulped some more, "God wants you to enjoy yourself. When you refuse to enjoy yourself you offend Her." Gloria was starting to riff. She would hit a vein in the conversation and dive in to mine it, throwing out rocks and gems and then more and more gems with no room for any edgewise words. Robbie didn't like it. Didn't like being demoted from participant to observer. It was as if she were in a play and her undelivered lines were snatched out from under her. Mid-scene Gloria turned a dialogue into a monologue and Robbie had nothing to do but stand like scenery or fifth-wheel it to the wings. Yet she wasn't onstage and she couldn't just walk away when someone was talking to her. She felt bullied. At least Gloria was entertaining enough that Robbie could enjoy and not enjoy at the same time.

"You should meet Massimo. I can't believe you haven't met. I have to introduce you," Robbie said. Gloria didn't even acknowledge the offer. She was on another of her rolls. Secretly, Robbie believed that Gloria had smoked so much dope as a living she'd never not be high. Good Lord, Gloria could talk. She was saying:

"Living is practice for Heaven. Heaven is like a big jazz hall with everybody grooving together. You have to have some basic skills before you can sit in. Without practice you can't play. Have fun. Wake up and smell the dope.

"What's up with you? You still miss life? Get over it. What was it about your life you loved so much?"

"Some of it wasn't bad."

"What part? I've been listening to you and it sounds like the people around you were cutthroat.

You're too nice. I would have been good at dealing with those people. I'd have killed them. I'd rather go to jail than let people shit on me the way they shit on you."

"Some of it was good."

Gloria didn't answer. Her pale eyes stared in. There was something in Robbie that Gloria didn't want in there. Robbie let her think.

"You know what?" Gloria said, "You should stop pretending you were dealing with good people. You're not being true to yourself. If you think someone's an asshole, they did something to deserve it. Own your bad opinions of them. That's what was wrong in your stories. No bad guys. You had too many excuses for everybody.

"I'm not saying you couldn't write. Your language was beautiful. But you never let your reader get righteously mad at anyone. That's not goodness. It's indecision. I don't mean to be mean, but I can't lie about the craft."

"Ouch. And I forgive you for hurting me."

"No you don't. But you will. And you won't make me suffer while you're mad at me. That's the nice part about your niceness. And don't think I don't take advantage of it."

When, in late mornings, Bartalemeo Mio dragged his easel inside the fence at the Sheep Meadow, Ivan was there waiting, hands clasped between his knees, beatific grin on his face. He'd sit there all day, watching, folded, rear on his heels, his thighs to his chest, his knees to his shoulders. When the light began to leave and Bartalemeo Mio stood to pack up, Ivan trailed the beautiful young man to the edges of the park, then returned to the meadow to stretch out and breathe deep in the grass where Bartalemeo Mio had been.

He was glad when Bartalemeo Mio stayed past sunset one night. Ivan sat, only a foot away from Bartalemeo Mio while the sky turned from blue to pink to purple to black. Rodents passed in the grass. The men, one living, one wraith, sat together, silent.

"Maybe we'll spend the night together. Maybe I'll see what he looks like when he's sleeping. Whether he moves about, climbing mountains in his sleep as he did when he was a baby in his carriage. Maybe he's still as a mummy in a tomb." Ivan wondered these things to himself. Was he tempted to speak to Bartalemeo Mio? To kiss him and perhaps be kissed by him? To know what went on in his head? Yes, indeed. Ivan was afraid to frighten the beauty. What reason had he to think that once encountering a ghost, Bartalemeo Mio would continue to return? None. He kept his peace and held his happiness like a firefly inside his hand.

Funny (strange, not ha ha) that Ivan would consider that Bartalemeo Mio might sleep still as a mummy in a tomb, for the artist, was, in his own mind, in a tomb, watching the door slide shut. From moment to moment Bartalemeo Mio switched back and forth from trying to figure out how to keep the door from closing to giving in. What was the use? He had no money. The paints he had he'd stolen. Chatting up salesgirls in art supply stores, he slipped cobalt blue into his cargo pockets. Nice girls. He didn't like to deceive them, but a tub of chromium was more important than being honest with a girl who wanted to be kind. They'd whisper to him, "These will be on sale next week. Thirty percent off." Or, "Come back at 5:30 when my manager leaves and I'll ring them up with my discount."

"See you then." He'd smile his dreamy, grateful, promising smile and slide a tube of cadmium yellow between the pages of his sketchpad. He knew where the mirrors were in Art Brown's and that if he was talking to sales help the watchers wouldn't pay him much attention. He had been blessed with a major talent and he had a responsibility to develop it. He had other blessings, too, he knew. A strong face, young and nicely put together. His legs were long, his calves were thick, his shoulders were square, his waist was a narrow oval. The high roundness of his rear showed through his jeans. All these to him were the support team for the painting. The painting was the thing. He told himself there was something noble in his stealing. He wove elaborate philosophies about sacrificing his honor, his ego, his self-respect for the sake of the painting. The romance of it appealed to him. There was rightness to his story as the starving, monumental artist giving himself up for art. It had balance, color and emotion. And the story could extend to his eventual, no quick, success.

Except his painting was suffering. Painting was getting harder for him. Even the easy things, a copse of trees blossoming white beyond the green meadow, a quick likeness of a friend, things that had been for years little more than parlor tricks to him were struggles now. The results were false, the feeling untrue, the look not so much amateur as hack. He cringed at the title. Hack. He should go ahead and move to a seaside town and paint the ocean with seagulls flying over. That'd be Mondays. And Tuesdays he'd turn out oceans with little dot boats on the horizon. He pulled a pencil nub from his pocket and sketched one, quick in the dark. Not bad. He hoisted his easel and bag.

Ivan dogged Bartalemeo Mio's steps, sometimes traveling beside him, watching the breeze play in his hair, behind him, enjoying the rhythm of his glutei, in front of him, glinding backwards, to worry over the furrow above his adored one's eyebrows.

"Bartalemeo Mio is unhappy." The thought welled up and shoved Ivan backwards. He hopped out of Bartalemeo Mio's way. "He's unhappy and untidy, not neat the way he used to be. Look how his nails are long. Are his teeth yellowing, or is it the light? His feet, they're callused and dry. They're still shapely, but they're in bad shape. He's dying from the bottom up." Ivan's heart cried. It was still crying long after Bartalemeo Mio turned out of the park and disappeared into the orderly network of streets and avenues.

"What was wrong with me that I didn't see the boy's pain? I was so glad to have him back that I wasn't seeing him. What was I so happy about? A face? A body? A memory? Did I let the memory supplant the real? Tomorrow I must pay attention to him. He's back, and I've been busy watching myself. What a fool." Ivan prayed for Bartalemeo Mio.

"Dear God, ruler of Heaven and Earth, protect the boy. Keep his talent dear to him, keep his life charmed. Make his days bright, his nights joyous, his laugh untouched by sadness. Make him never be a disappointment to himself. Keep him strong. Give him happiness." Anything was worth a try.

Robbie introduced Massimo and Gloria, finally. Already, Gloria didn't like Massimo much. Self-important, arrogant, probably a welfare pimp in his life, and, of course, he took up a lot of Robbie's time.

Robbie, although she arranged it, wasn't wholly in favor of this meeting; she liked keeping each to herself; she liked the jealously each grew in the other. Still, it was the polite thing to do, she had to. Funny thing was, they could have met anytime, and not through Robbie, without any effort at all. It was almost more effort not to meet.

Introductions took place in the island of sunny daffodils down from Boys' Gate at 100th Street. Robbie and Massimo glinded together from the top of the Great Hill at 106th. Gloria was already there, making a poem in her mind. Yellow light reflected off the flowers under her chin and the hollows of her eyes, and the bottoms of her arms. She rested in a faint halo of light.

"Massimo, Gloria. Gloria, Massimo. You're so lucky you got here after Massimo did. The Fauves used to rout wraiths out of their sleeping places. They don't any more, 'cause Massimo's teaching them better.

"Massimo, Gloria is a famous writer and bon vivant. I don't know if you have a lot in common; Gloria will stretch your world. Gloria stretches everybody's world."

Robbie felt excluded as Massimo and Gloria stared each other down. And what did they see? Robbie could almost hear their thoughts, Massimo thinking:

"High yellow bitch. Who does she think she is looking at me like I don't have a right to be in the same world? Is she baring her teeth? Doesn't she know adults don't stick out their bottom lips like children? She *is* baring her teeth. Probably growls. I bet if I started at her she'd jump and run. Nah, I'm not going to do that; it'd be fun though." That would be Massimo as he gripped Robbie's hand.

Robbie bet Gloria was thinking, "Reminds me of my old boyfriend Andre. It's the sensitive men who beat their wives. 'Nobody understands me.' Stroking his beard like he has the right to judge me. Well, I'm judging you, too, motherfucker. I bet you're hiding a weak chin under that beard."

Massimo and Gloria both began talking at the same time.

"Pleased..."

"Pleased..."

"You go."

"No, you. Please."

"Pleased to meet you."

"Pleased to meet you."

"I don't know why it's taken me so long to get you two together," Robbie smiled.

Gloria was lying. Gloria didn't lie for the reasons most people lied, to protect the other person's feelings, to keep the peace, to make somebody else, or herself feel good, to suck up to build a relationship. Gloria lied because she liked it. For her a lie was an act of creation, of making something whole and new out of bits and clues and feelings and whims. Rather like a witch with eye of toad and tail of newt, Gloria knew her creations were powerful. She took pride in their sturdy construction. They always had their spark of brilliance. Lying made her present in a way that simply reporting did not.

Gloria didn't lie to protect her faults. She embraced them. She toyed with them like a loose tooth. She exposed them for a living. She'd made the fault of always choosing the wrong man into a play that had been applauded from coast to coast. The bigness – a fault – of her butt was the inspiration of her most anthologized monologue. (Actually, she liked her big butt. Sure from time to time she didn't like looking at it, but it was behind her and looking at it was something she had to go out of her way to do. Men liked her behind, or said they did. When they teased her about it, she knew they did it with patronal affection. If they complained about her big butt, it wasn't because they didn't like it, but because they didn't like her. When it happened, she knew it was time to move on, not that she always did. For a couple of guys she redoubled her cardio and hired a trainer. Inches left her rear end as surely as those men left her life. She took her not-as-big butt out to attract a new man. Or two. Or more. In life, she'd never lacked for men. Men were easy.)

"Actually, I'm not pleased to meet you at all. I wish there was no you. You take up way too much space in Robbie's mind and from what I can see, you don't deserve it." She said it just like that, without special energy, just making a neutral observation. All three of them felt their faces grow hot as if steam was building in their bodies and their valves were shut.

"I'll see you later, Robbie. I've got a game with the fellas." Massimo said. He kissed her with great show and left. He held his dignity intact; it was as palpable as another person, larger even than Massimo was; he and his dignity were like a couple as his legs marched him back up the drive.

"A glind is as distinctive as a walk," Robbie said.

"Aren't you going to say anything about what I said to him?" Gloria said.

"You were rude. You wonder what I see in him? Let me tell you, you had me wondering what I see in you. Why you picked this moment to be a drama queen, I don't know. If you and Massimo aren't going to be friends, fine. Can we talk about something else?" Robbie huffed ahead, and Gloria, surprised, had to catch up. Robbie never lorded over Gloria. Gloria's always teased Robbie for being a goody two-shoes and Robbie always tried to prove her cred, or change. But this time, Robbie told Gloria off. Robbie was offended. Or so it seemed. Even Robbie had to look closely to recognize that she was glad.

Massimo didn't like being dissed. Not at all. If he wasn't getting respect, he wasn't staying. He'd made the effort, for Robbie. There wasn't any need in his life, his after-life, for another woman. No. That wasn't true, not totally. He didn't need another woman, but he had been curious. Always interested in meeting another woman. He laughed at himself. He'd been interested, and then he'd been embarrassed. Bitch dissing him served him right.

But that Gloria was much. He'd expected admiration for him, envy for Robbie. He was well built, good-looking, had something meaningful going on. He was used to impressing his girlfriends' girlfriends. He enjoyed the tension of forbidden desire. Meeting his girlfriends' girlfriends upset the balance in his romantic relationships in his favor. Meeting him prompted conversations that began, "Girl, if he wasn't your man..." Or to a third party, "She better watch her step. 'Cause the minute she says she's not interested, my hat is in the ring." Or from the really hungry, "She don't know what she's got; I know how to treat a man like that." Not that he was ever tempted by that. Girlfriends who treated their girlfriends like shit treated their boyfriends like shit. He knew about these conversations. All he had to do was ask, "What did your girlfriend say about me?" This time he didn't care.

It's a good thing he didn't ask. If he had, Robbie wouldn't have had anything to say unless she made it up. All afternoon Robbie and Gloria wandered the Sheep Meadow making up stories about people relaxing under the mid-season sun.

An improvisation from Gloria: "She's a ballet student recovering from broken foot. You can tell she's a dancer from the bun on her neck and the snooty way she holds her head. She's gained weight since she broke her foot and now she's afraid to go back to class. She'll be the fattest one there instead of Gertrude, who she always looked down on. Maybe Gertrude will now look down on her. She couldn't stand that, no. Better to give up dance altogether than to go back and be the person others compare themselves to when they want to feel better. That's why she's reading that book with the diagrams of body systems. She's thinking of becoming a nurse."

An ad lib from Robbie: "That boy over there is playing hooky. Every time a uniform goes by, he gets nervous. He hides his face. The truth is no one is looking for him. Nobody knows he's gone. He's such a goody-two-shoes nobody for a moment considers he's not where he ought to be. His teachers think he's home. His parents know he's at school. There's no reason to double-check. When he gets home tonight, he'll know he's gotten away with not going to school today. He won't be happy. He'll be disappointed. His mother will kiss him and give him a plate of potatoes and roast beef and broccoli; his father will ask him how school was today, and he'll lie. 'Okay,' he'll say, and that'll be fine with his father. He'll sleep poorly. He'll be here again tomorrow if it doesn't rain. He'll be here until his father yells at him."

"That guy in the shorts with the plaid cowboy shirt? He works at night. Doesn't like it. It's too different from everybody else. Especially it's different from his girlfriend. He's waiting for her now. He's got lunch for both of them in his knapsack. Lobster salad sandwiches from Zabar's," here Robbie and Gloria looked at each other and groaned, "and seedless green grapes and gin and tonic in a thermos. She may not even come – she couldn't promise she'd be here. He enjoyed planning the lunch for the possibility she might share it with him. Look, the weather is as beautiful as predicted, the leaves are tender, the grass is thick, and if I'm not mistaken, he's lighting a joint." Gloria was beside him in no time, her head over the smoke that rose from the joint and his nose and mouth. Sure enough, a woman does come. About his age, walking fast. Before she sits with him, she pulls a box of Teddy Grahams from her knapsack. The guy and the woman laugh about the cookies. Perfect with gin and tonic. "I'll tell you a secret about him," Gloria says. "He's got another girlfriend. She thinks he's at home sleeping."

That night Robbie and Massimo snuggled in their nest. Robbie liked the way he held fast to her in his sleep. She liked his face. How his eyelashes shone in the moonlight, the clear decisiveness of his nose. She'd known Massimo and Gloria wouldn't get along. Massimo was so goal-oriented. So determined. So neat. Such a Boy Scout. And Gloria? Gloria was no Brownie. She was sloppy. Not just in her appearance, but in her standards. Who was disgusting to her one week she was sleeping with the next. Robbie was grateful and proud to have created something so stable and so right with Massimo. She held him tight. In his sleep he smiled and yawned. Wraiths don't get bad breath in their sleep.

Autumn

In New York, autumn comes Labor Day night. Somewhere about three-thirty in the morning a cool breeze chills the city and people get out of their beds and rummage about their linen closets or cedar chests for blankets. By the time they awaken the sun will have upped and baked the chill away. But the possibility of cold will have reasserted itself inside New Yorkers. In Central Park, the people who had been away for the summer come back to their city schedules. Like daffodils in the Spring, they appear all at once and in profusion sporting the subdermal glow from long weekends in the Hamptons. Many of them come back on horseback, entering the park at 90th Street half a block from Claremont stables. The smell along the street from the stables was unmistakable. It gained fortitude along the bridle path inside the park. Wraiths love that smell simply because it's strong enough to penetrate a wraith's senses; it was a favorite spot for Ivan. "What is dearer to life than defecating?" He had rhapsodized when he introduced the spot to Robbie. "What could be more erotic than the smell of hot feces? Women go gaga over the smell of babies. I've never met a baby who didn't smell like poop or the threat of poop. You women pretend you don't like shit, but you do. Just like men." This was wallowing in its finest. Wallowing in homesickness for life, for living, for warmth and its fetidness. To howl, to moan, to get down into the stinking garbage and roll in the muck, drenched in the mad hustle, fighting worry by making plans. This was no fun alone. Though it was a nice spot, Robbie went there only with Ivan.

That morning it was particularly fine. A moment in which it was good to be. Strong sun diluted by cool shade, the auto traffic providing a hum that ebbed and flowed like ocean. Ivan was about to say something, but when The Duchess joined them, he stopped. Two riders passed beneath the wraiths' hanging legs, one rider in blue jeans and a plaid shirt, the other in breeches, jacket and hat.

"I love this time of year," Ivan said, his arms flung out wide like Julie Andrews singing *The Sound of Music.* Shit in his nostrils always made him very dramatic.

The Duchess said, "Central Park is so much nicer when the crowds die down. One can't really appreciate the park until after Labor Day. It's just too crowded in summer. The people who really belong here go away during the high season. It's the same everywhere. We can't stand the crowds." Winken, Blinken and Nod were trailing her. "This summer, though, I've been so busy with the children. It's hard with triplets, you know, to let each of them know that he's loved just as much as the others. I have to keep track of who got fed first the last time, and rotate. Oh, you can let your eyebrows down. They don't eat really, of course not. We play act." Seneca, last in the entourage, rolled her bright eyes in her dark face.

"Thank goodness I don't have triple diapers to deal with. Living mothers must have a devil of a time. It was so much fun teaching the babies to void."

She clapped her gloved hands together and the babies lined up shoulder to shoulder, elevated and levitated in the air, their round heads, round stomachs and stumpy penises facing the sky. All spurted pee, looking like an elaborate but inefficient sprinkler. While still peeing, the synchronized babies then twisted over to face down, turned back to face up, then stood, glinding shoulder to shoulder once again.

"That's really disgusting, Duchess." Ivan said. Robbie nearly fell off the bridge laughing.

Of all the seasons, Robbie liked autumn least, despite its spectacular days. Like slow death, the best it could do, with its dwindling resources, was to promise to daily creep toward winter, which at least had serenity to recommend it. Autumn was too much an old man at a party trying to be like the young men, doing the dances the young men do, without the nonchalance or natural grace; autumn was almost embarrassing in its showiness, and more than a little sad. Too-bright leaves dropped dead on the ground were crushed under live feet. Pathetic.

"I like the summer. But the park's best season is six o'clock every morning," Robbie said. And indeed, it did seem the group that came earliest, the birdwatchers, was the happiest. Rarely was a birdwatcher anything but excited, expectant and joyous, crunching around in the earliest smudge of light, their pant legs damp at the cuffs.

"Ungodly," countered The Duchess. "I never get up 'til ten."

"Oh, come off it," Ivan said. "If we could sleep more than two hours at a time, being here wouldn't seem so much of an eternity." He rolled his eyes skyward. "She wants us to spend as much time as possible contemplating our transgressions so that we can correct them and join Her in Heaven, where everyone is perfect, unlike us sinners down here. Who, not so incidentally, pretend to need sleep like the livings so that it makes us seems like the livings. You're not fooling anybody."

"Just because your soul is tormented doesn't mean we all suffer," The Duchess said.

"If you slept an hour in the last century, it'd be a lot," Ivan said. The Duchess rose and left, babies bouncing in her wake, Seneca pulling up the rear.

Ivan dusted his hands together with satisfaction. "I thought she'd never leave. I've had my dream." Two more would come soon and Ivan would ascend to Heaven.

The good thing about good things happening to your friends is you get to share their joy. That's the theory. Robbie was jealous and angry. She swept them politely under a falsely cheerful curiosity.

"What was it like?"

"Beautiful. Blue clouds with lavender undersides, baby blue sky, ancient Grecian garments in antique white. Kind of cliché, really. But whoever put it together had a sense of humor.

"How do you know you're not the one who put it together?"

"I was fighting it. I knew this was the first dream, and I don't know why, but I was fighting it. I fought it so hard I woke up. I voided. I took a run down to the Ramble and spied on a couple of lovers. By the time I went back to sleep, I'd forgotten all about the dream. Damn if it didn't pick up right where it'd left off."

"I'd hope it'd be more like Jamaica. Or the Tahiti of my imagination."

"Maybe it is. I've heard that the dream changes, the first one is just an introductory."

She thought about him leaving. That he'd be gone and she'd still be in the park. She wondered what he had that she didn't have. Why God found Ivan worthy. Ivan was vain, selfish, totally self-centered and manipulative while she herself was trying so hard to be good. To do the right things. Say the correct words. Strike down the ugly feelings. She said: "Whom do you have to screw to get out of this place?" She tried to make it sound like a joke, but her voice cracked.

"I guess it's best to hit everyone, just in case."

Robbie didn't know why Ivan had bothered to be so hush-hush about telling her. By the next day it was common knowledge.

"Did you hear about Ivan?" One questioned.

"Yeah," Another answered.

"He can't wait to get his ass outta here. Don't you usually wait until your third dream before you tell folks?" A third opined.

"When I get my dreams, I'm going to wake people up and crow, 'So long, suckers.'" A fourth joked.

The Duchess pulled Robbie aside and said, "People tell you what they're like and you ignore them, or think somehow, they won't be that way with you. A charming young man will confess he's an awful womanizer and the lady to whom he confesses is dizzy with shock when he has carnal knowledge of other women. A friend tells one she's competitive, yet one is hurt when one's friend competes with one. People are who they are."

Spring

Ivan's party was a dream. It had taken two seasons for Ivan to have all three of his dreams and it was spring in the park again. Daffodils were crowding each other along the drive at 100th Street. Tender green was breaking hard dirt. Night was still coming early, so the party could begin early. Preparations were simply to tell Conchita and her rhythm group where and when to show up and then tell everybody else.

The Duchess came. It was her first non-voyage in decades and she arrived amidst her own to-do, changed. She had acquired grace and moved now, if not with rhythm, then at least without awkwardness. Still a bony bird of a woman, her presence was now plump and warm. The triplets floated about The Duchess' knees, on all fours. When they dropped into sitting position they hovered near The Duchess' ankles, half a foot or so above ground. They, too, were no longer scrawny and each was draped with jewels; strings of pearls hung off their chubby shoulders, their fat wrists twisted with rubies. They slurped and burped deliciously on the stones, stringing plenteous spit on their treasures. Resting an ungloved hand on Robbie's arm, The Duchess whispered into Robbie's ear that she too had had a dream. Robbie kissed her. Her cheek was dry and soft.

"Really, Duchess! How wonderful for you." Again Robbie felt the sting of envy. What was so special about The Duchess that she'd been chosen to go to Heaven? What secret had she discovered?

"I'll tell you, my little angels have acquainted me with true happiness. Heaven is almost superfluous for me now, although I would like a friendlier climate for the babies. Of course they're coming with me. They were in my dream, and each one wore a little crown made of blue roses. So cute! I refuse to believe in a God who'd put my babies in my non-voyage dream and then leave them behind. God wouldn't do that."

"Of course not," Robbie said. She was trying to believe in a God that didn't send dreams that wouldn't come true. She admired The Duchess' certainty.

"Where is that Ivan?" The Duchess steamed toward the party boy, the triplets following her like cartoons floating on an aroma, like Gloria floating on weed smoke. Her servant lingered behind. Seneca looked very young without The Duchess' shadow lying over her.

"Are you going to Heaven, too?" Robbie said.

"No." She said it quietly, defiantly, bedecked in a lustrous rope of round pearls, rubbing the bottom of the loop between her child-sized fingers. "I'm not ready for my dreams." She was a curious being, small like The Duchess, but not as young as her size would first indicate.

"How long have you been here?"

"Since before The Duchess."

"But she's been here since before the park was even finished."

"I was here before then. I died in a riot to keep our homes."

"Seneca. Of course."

"Yes." She wasn't used to speaking and she was careful what she said "My father owned a store downtown. We were free and owned our homes. Bought the land and built the houses. Nice houses. Not like the Irish who lived in the shanties. My father said they lived worse than slaves. Frederick Douglass stayed at our house one night. My father angered him when he said that. I remember how Mr. Douglass said 'No life is worse than slavery," his funny hair quivering.

Robbie was fascinated. Seneca had known Frederick Douglass? Here was a woman with many afternoons-full of stories to tell.

"I want you to meet Gloria, she's my friend the. . ."

"I know who she is."

"Can I introduce you?"

"We've met."

Gloria looked up then, across the room with Ivan, and waved Robbie over.

Ivan kissed the babies one by one, like a doting uncle. "I do believe happiness has replaced your hauteur," he said to the Duchess.

"Yes, it's true," The Duchess said. "I'm happy. I have a little announcement to make. I too have been having my dreams. Any time now, I'll be leaving this dear place and taking my babies with me." They grinned toothlessly up at her face, gurgling and cooing, she gurgling and cooing back. It was hard to tell in which direction affection was flowing hardest. "You may think I've forgotten that I owe you," the Duchess said, "but I haven't."

"I never thought you'd forgotten," Ivan said.

"Don't worry. Be happy." The Duchess lifted her scrawny elbows by her narrow face. She unclasped the necklaces. “All yours,” she said. “These, and the rest of them.”

Bartalemeo Mio stared for a long while at his canvas of a view looking from the Sheep Meadow. There was Tavern on the Green with its fanciful hedges, traffic on the drive, horse-drawn carriages, cyclists, brave and tiny runners in their bright shorts and shirts. Peace and green inside the fence. His canvas of many greens. The grass was green and blue and gray and specks of yellow and red. The trees were green with white on the undersides of their outer leaves. The air was a bright acid green, spring-like in its intensity. Bartalemeo Mio wanted this painting to sing the greens. He wanted the breeze to saunter through his grass; he wanted the sun to polka in the air. He wanted the buildings on Central Park West to feel like the velvet lining of the box that held the jewel that was Central Park. Instead the whole thing looked dead.

Bartalemeo Mio’s romantic notion of the starving artist was dead, too. To do art, one must be absolutely secure. The act of creation can’t coexist with the experience of doubt. That is why an artist needs food and sleep in a safe, clean place on a daily, dependable basis. Plus pocket money; enough to catch a bus, or buy a drink, or a ticket to a movie. An artist must know material security. Luxury, even. It’s the only way, not counting drugs, he can make the awful, heart-flipping leap into not knowing. Who can say what Van Gogh might have done if he lived more like Monet who painted masterpieces daily and entertained in the dining room of his house-proud wife. Bartalemeo Mio was mightily insecure.

Every now and then, music from the carousel rose and went.

Bartalemeo Mio packed up. He was ashamed of his painting. His face burned when strollers stopped to look, comparing what he saw when he looked to what they saw when they looked. He didn't want to be identified with the vision on his canvas. He stomped to a trash bin and bent the painting inside. A covey of young sunbathers moved away from him. A garbage picker took the painting from the can a very few minutes later. Bartalemeo Mio knew it wouldn't sell.

"Don't waste your strength," he wanted to tell the garbage picker. Not wanting to draw more attention to himself, he kept silent.

When the sky went dark, Ivan followed Bartalemeo Mio north to the Ramble. By night the Ramble, a place men go to couple with men, is exciting or shabby depending on one's outlook. Men, not always the most young and beautiful, or even the most confident, stroll for partners, they fuck/suck, and move on. Bartalemeo Mio found someone whose dick was hard, and on his knees, Bartalemeo Mio serviced the man. When our artist asked for money, the man knocked him to the ground and held Bartalemeo Mio's perfect face in the dirt with his knee, which he gyrated on Bartalemeo Mio's head for some time. Hard granules ground between our boy's inside lips and gums, they grew soft on his tongue. He didn't fight. He covered where he could. He closed his eyes and waited. He saw, when he opened his eyes, a large stone shining green in the dark, and even as the aggressor abused him, Bartalemeo Mio stretched out his arm and wrapped his fingers tight around the Duchess' center emerald which Ivan had placed for him.

Are you wondering if this counted as interfering in the world of the livings? Were the rules that a wraith couldn't give gifts to livings, even if the wraith didn't expose himself? Yes. Yes, they were. Even though Ivan didn't show himself, it broke the rules for Heaven. The damage to the rules was no greater when Bartalemeo Mio found another gem, a diamond about twenty clear carats and quite gaudily gorgeous. That was two days after the night incident at the Ramble. The day in between, Bartalemeo Mio hadn't come to the park. Ivan waited for him all day. He imagined his young artist at a pawnbroker, or maybe Macy's Estate Jewelry Appraisal department; that was easier. Ivan had never been to a pawnbroker but he had sold some jewelry at Macy's. He hoped Bartalemeo Mio was bathing, perhaps getting a manicure, a pedicure. He thought of the deliciousness of a massage, and hoped for one for Bartalemeo Mio. He pictured his beloved's neck exposed, his multitudinous curls heavy with water and shampoo, his sections of scalp rotating under a washer's strong fingertips. This too, he wished for Bartalemeo Mio, along with new pants in a soft, pre-washed cotton, sweaters light and airy that would drape over his broad shoulders and slip and shift on his chest. Ivan imagined Bartalemeo Mio eating steak and potatoes and asparagus and key lime pie and was glad.

Everybody knew what he'd done. Even the Fauves avoided him. The only wraith whose opinion he cared about was Robbie's. "You're a careful thinker. Are you horrified?"

But Robbie wasn't. She said, "I'm excited. Amazed." Ivan always seemed to her emotionally cool. Distant from feelings. Amused by them. Robbie shook her head. No. Not horrified at all. "I think you have passion, and where there's passion, there's no choice."

"Well, well, you're not the terrified little suck-approval I thought you were." He tousled her hair. Her soul purred. She'd been jealous that he was going to Heaven and now she was jealous that he wasn't.

The morning Bartalemeo Mio returned to the Sheep Meadow and then found the diamond, he talked while he set up. "All the while I was cocksucking, I had my eyes open. I saw his hairs, close and closer, the dull gleam of his zipper, and especially the ground. I knew the ground very well. I knew where every cigarette butt was. I saw every wrinkled condom. The heel prints. Dead leaves. I used my painter's eyes to see it all. That emerald wasn't there. When it was there, I saw it. I can't see you, but I know you're there." It was the same speech he'd delivered to the air at the Ramble that morning before he came to the Sheep Meadow. He talked all day.

"I've known I'm an artist all my life. As a child, the games my mother got for me bored me. After a while she stopped buying things to entertain me that I couldn't make something with. She wanted me to be an engineer. The rules in engineering are unbendable. That doesn't interest me.

"My morals aren't so strong. I have done things with full awareness that they were the wrong things. Perhaps I can buy my morals back with your gifts.

"Do you think it takes wealth to be moral? I don't. But I don't understand about the camel and the eye of the needle, either. Do you know how much money I got for the emerald? A fortune. I have a friend at Sotheby's, so I didn't get ripped off. I would have been easy to cheat. I was amazed at the amount of money my friend mentioned as possible. Then he was able to get me more.

"I got an apartment and took in a roommate. A guy from my class at the Art Students' League. The only time he painted was at class. Now, instead of tending bar at night and sleeping days, he'll paint days and sleep nights. He'll tend bar on weekends only. I don't think he'll be one of the greats, but he does.

"He doesn't have to pay me rent. I'll buy the food for both of us. He must clean up after himself. I could have a cleaner come in, but it is important that I clean up after myself. We'll do our own laundry. Wash our own dishes. Spray and wipe our own bathrooms. I like my roommate well enough; he is pleasant, but we aren't friends. I don't think we'll see each other much. Maybe in winter. I offered him half an apartment rent-free because he was struggling and I could help him.

"I bought the girl I was living with a convertible couch. She's kind, and now she can share her apartment without sharing her bed."

Bartalemeo Mio worked on a new canvas, painting quickly, shapes emerging like in a Polaroid. "I am making a portrait of myself. Someday it will hang in a major private collection and someday after that it will hang in a museum." Bartalemeo Mio was painting himself in a late Renaissance style as a saint at the moment of being blessed by God. He had a mirror than hung lopsidedly off his easel. "My mother paid for violin lessons for me when I was little. The music school was way on the West Side in a beat-up brownstone. We took a bus uptown, then across town. The people over there were dark, and they spoke Spanish and in the summer there were men with blocks of ice to shave and put flavoring in to make ices my mother wouldn't buy for me.

"My lessons were in a room that might have once been a bathroom. It was tiled halfway up the walls. It was on the fifth floor and had a skylight. I loved that school. My dreams incubated there. In the halls I heard music. Piano, clarinet, violin. Over and over, the same passages repeated, the same songs from the pianos, working out the mistakes like a masseuse pushing a kink from a muscle. My mother waited for me on the second floor in a parlor with complicated plaster in the ceiling and folding metal chairs and a folding metal table. When my lesson was over I was supposed to go to the second floor to meet her, but every Saturday morning I stayed outside my lesson room listening. My mother always climbed the extra three flights of steps to get me. For that reason she was angry with me whenever we passed the men with the ices. So she never bought one for me.

(Summer)

"My dream was to be a violinist. I could picture myself in a velvet suit, with my chin doubled on the shiny surface of my violin. My violin spoke for me, at least in my dreams. It was tiny and mournful. It could sing happy songs, but there was something in its voice that betrayed the sadness underneath. Not a very good actor, the violin. Happy went against its nature. I liked that about it. My relationship with my violin mirrored my mother's relationship with me. I could do happy, that was what she wanted to see, but I was my true self when I was melancholy. At the playground I liked sitting next to my mother on a bench listening to another mother cry about how they couldn't afford to go to Europe this summer, or that they were wrestling with whether to ask for a scholarship or send the child to public school, both unthinkable options. I was a nosy little boy. I learned the clues to a husband's affair a wife would recognize: matches in his pockets from restaurants they'd never gone to together, in a neighborhood he had no reason to be; or his clothing smelled like perfume, or he had starting eating cottage cheese and lettuce. The tone in the voices that told these stories, there was always a tone beneath the anger, there was a tone that vibrated in my chest that filled me deeply to overflowing.

"Am I boring you?"

"NO!" Ivan wanted to shout.

"I'm just babbling. I want you to know that I know you're there. Aren't you?"

Ivan was in no way bored. Amused, certainly. Confused, perhaps. Ivan sat cross-legged at Bartalemeo Mio's workstation. He remembered Bartalemeo Mio as a young boy. It was not a melancholy child attached to his mother's side that Ivan called to mind. Bartalemeo Mio had been, not to put too fine a point on it, bad. His bottom was swatted with regularity and never without reason. His answer to those spankings was more than likely to be running off and doing some more of whatever he'd been doing. The spankings were received in the same good-hearted way that they were given, no more than punctuations in the game little Bartalemeo Mio, on his chubby legs, threw himself into, yelling with the other, less beautiful, children.

"Paintings nearly spilled out of me. I never got my adult-sized violin. I grew out of it at just the right time. The child-sized one, my little treasure, I had until a month or two ago. I sold it. I wonder if I could buy it back, if it's still there?" Excitement grew. "I don't need it. I don't play. It's nice to have, though.

"Too much green in my hair, do you think?" Bartalemeo Mio considered his canvas. It looked like he'd look if he were green and gold. "No, no, I don't think so either."

"Now wait a blessed minute!" Ivan wanted to say. There was too much green in the hair.

"I like the green. I don't know where these notions come from. You paint what you see, yes, but from where is the vision? Why did I see green just now? My mother's hair was black, pure black. You know what that means? There is some black DNA somewhere in her, and therefore in me. There's no such thing as pure black hair in the Caucasian race, you know? Ergo. We Italians are probably all an eighth Moorish anyway, Italy being so close to Africa. 'The Niggers of Europe.' That's how we're seen over there. My mother, may she rest in peace, would die if she heard me say that. She'd die if she heard me say nigger. And she'd die again to hear suggest she had black blood. May she rest in peace."

Even on the roof of the American Wing, where Gloria and Robbie sat, their legs hanging over the edge, was hot.

"Do you think we could fly?" Robbie asked. "We don't touch the ground when we walk, could we defy gravity altogether?"

"We can do anything," Gloria said.

But it was Robbie that tried. Robbie stood up. Gloria prayed. She liked looking at Robbie. Looking at Robbie made Gloria embarrassed to have rejoiced in being light-skinned. "Not that I could have passed for white, or ever wanted to, except perhaps as an experiment, but I was glad I wasn't dark. Robbie is brown. Nut brown. Warm mother brown. A definite, unmistakable, got it in the first look no question Negro brown, not like my skin, pale and undecided, neither black or white, not warm, not cold, not especially pretty, even in candlelight, dead in yellow light. Her skin is a color to roll around on my tongue, a sweet, round, soft color…" These are the things Gloria thought as Robbie stood on the edge of the glass roof. Robbie thought of flying. She stretched her arms out above her head, alongside her ears.

"Superman!" She gulped and leapt. She rose up a little and floated forward. As hard and as sustained as she could, Gloria blew air up, to get and keep Robbie afloat. She imagined herself the wind. "If I believe in her flight, it can happen," she thought. So she breathed with all the fire and force of the yoga she'd practiced for years. Robbie in the meantime abandoned the Clark Kent method and was flapping her arms when she crashed into one of the trees just to the north of the museum. You can see it from the bus right when it turns from Fifth Avenue onto the transverse.

Robbie's skin was scraped from the knee, and although it didn't hurt, her ankle hung lopsided when she glinded home to Massimo. Robbie had been proud of her legs. As a living, she'd worn skirts and high heels when she'd wanted extra leverage in her negotiations. Running, biweekly waxing, rubbing concealer and foundation on the dark spots below her knees where she'd picked off the scabs as a child. Now the skin on her right leg was scaly for half its length. Massimo kissed it and kissed it from top to toe. He confessed it his favorite spot on her body. Where his hand rested. "I believe you're a scar man," Robbie said, and she called the damage "My badge of happiness." By which she meant courage.

"You took a big chance." Massimo hugged her.

Massimo loved baseball, so Robbie got into it. As a living, Robbie hadn't been a baseball fan. Every once in a while the living Robbie watched a piece of a game. She didn't get it. Baseball demanded knowing the history of the players, and by the time Robbie thought she might bother, it was too late. Back in the pre-expansion sixties, she could have learned all the players, but by the time Robbie figured out that knowing baseball would make her a more attractive date, there were too many teams to learn, too many players. Mantis. Mays. Marris. Yastremski. Kaline. Gibson. Koufax. Clemente. These names were magic to the initiates. All Robbie remembered was a vague story about wife-swapping. After death she began to appreciate baseball as a clock and a calendar, a way of keeping track of history. Baseball was an intricate mechanism in which men aged, mostly with grace, mostly with the shadow of who they once were carried neatly inside them. It called for specific skills, respectfully applied by union players, each responsible for his bit of work. And when they all did their work well, they all prospered. The pitcher did not have to be a good runner. In fact, being a good pitcher usually interfered with the ability to run. Every once in a while there was a player who was good at everything. But such players were rare and almost always young. Parts give out. In baseball, wisdom battles exuberance, mind masters muscle, studying beats instinct. Sometimes.

Under Massimo's tutelage Robbie became a connoisseur of the high tight and inside. A critic of the dipping swing. A chronicler of the season's bests and worsts. And a lover of the generosity of baseball fans. A guy comes out of the dugout in his first World Series and hits a grand slam. The crowd is wild for him from that single play. Yet a single bad play couldn't topple a player from reverence. Once the greatness in a player was exhibited, he could slump for years before fans would dump him, and they would always remember and admire his seasons of glory. Or perhaps what grabbed Robbie's fancy after she died was the Broadway Show League.

The Broadway Show League plays in Central Park all summer. The teams are the actors and crew of any show on Broadway. The competition is fierce. *Cats* goes nine innings against *The Lion King*. *The King and I* overrules *Les Misérables*. *Hamlet vs. Streamers*. *The Piano Lesson* against *The Sound of Music*. You should have seen the game when the boys in *A Chorus Line* made grand jetés home. That particular Friday Meatloaf's band was playing *Honor*. The bleachers were mostly empty. Probably a big holiday weekend, Robbie thought. Room enough for the wraiths to take seats. Gloria sat between Rodrigo and Ivan, Robbie on the other side of Ivan and Massimo on the other side of Robbie. Massimo kept complaining about the Fauves not coming down to the games. You could get right next to the managers and know what the signals were, hang out with the teams if you wanted, so long as you stayed out of the way. A Meatloaf player knocked a ball out of the field. Meatloaf always wins, had for as long as Ivan could remember. The Meatloaf team was all ringers; the show had never been on Broadway, hadn't toured in years. But boy, those guys could play.

Robbie squinted at the sun in her face, felt the cool shade on her back, the heat from the bleachers, dust rising like dirty halos around the players. The sounds clear and long, the swack of a strong bat against a speeding ball sharp and hard and then echoing on. One could meditate in the space of that echo on this: the ball could be tricky, the ball could dip and pretend, but the bat had to be straight and true, and wasn't that what made that swack so sweet? The sound of a victory of plain honesty. Jane Alexander was at bat. (Robbie could argue the other way, too. That a bat is a large instrument for the protection of a small area and only a ball of relentless focus can pass through. That was the thing about baseball.)

Meatloaf won. Afterwards everybody who had been at the game went with Gloria to meditate. It was that kind of afternoon, long and lazy, and baseball made the mood. Gloria sat on the ground with her legs pressed open, the rest followed suit, all in a loose circle, Robbie and Massimo near to each other, Rodrigo slightly apart, Ivan with his face to the sun. "Ivan catches the light like an angel," Robbie thought as she closed her eyes. Gloria prayed:

"Dear God, let me do Our work today. I know that I have a purpose and that I have exactly the tools I need to accomplish it. I know that with the right tools any job is easy. Therefore, I will not struggle, I will not force myself.

"I forgive myself for running for cover in the opinions of others. Seeking quorums and majorities rather than being clear in myself. Today I do not seek the counsel of others. Today I stand in the open universe of my own beliefs and blessings. I trust myself." Robbie felt a door to a room in which she'd been welcome closing. Would the opinions Gloria used to solicit now be intrusions? "In this moment I clean my house, the windows and the corners. The closets and the floors. The sink and the toilet." The scent of bathroom cleaner wafted in Robbie's memory. She had liked the smells of clean. Wood soap. Pine. There were parts of mopping she'd liked. Hands in bright yellow rubber gloves thrust down into warm, scented water. The way a room looked as she mopped herself out the door with the final damp rinse. She liked the feeling of having brought cleanliness and order to a space. She liked hanging newly washed, dried and folded towels onto a towel bar where the wall had been wiped down with cleanser and then a fresh-water sponge, and a lick to the towel bar, too. She liked a room recently cared for with soapy water and elbow grease. "Today I welcome the comforting light of freshness throughout me." Gloria breathed. "I am one with all Gods. I am floating, flying, supported by Love, and part of Love. Amen."

Robbie opened her eyes. Massimo was still, his eyes open. Robbie thought he looked entranced, and considered the word, playing with it in her mind. A funny word, entranced. Entrance. Had he been entered?

It was quiet for a while. The trellis above the Conservatory Garden was always empty. This afternoon, it was hot. Gloria unbuttoned her blouse and held it open to catch a tiny breeze, no bigger than a lizard. Her breasts were large and round, her ribs frail in comparison. Her blouse wafted out behind her. Robbie closed her eyes. Sometimes Gloria rode Roberta's very last nerve.

"No one can accuse you of not starring in your own show," Ivan said.

So here's the truth: Gloria blew Massimo away. Her determined hair, her ready laugh. Her frowns and scowls were ready, too, but the laugh was never too far away, and its sound was the sound of cymbals and bells and trumpets heralding the arrival of Fun. He was afraid of her, too, a woman who spoke her mind. Her formidable mind, her seductive roundness, her sweet softness, her hard and muscular temper, where did she keep it all? She was not a big person compared to himself, yet her parts, each alone was massive in his mind. Her breasts were planets. Such a woman he'd never known before and such a woman was very convincing, could drive him from his own center to hover around hers, turn him into an acolyte at a church where she was the minister. No one he'd known in life had prepared him for the onslaught of so much smart femaleness.

They went on dates. They rowed on the lake, they smooched in the moonlight at Belvedere Castle. When Denzel Washington did Richard III at the Delacorte, Gloria swooned to tease Massimo, who was jealous, for Gloria and Denzel had been passing friends when Gloria was alive. Theatre wasn't Massimo's world even a little bit. Massimo's rendition of Shakespeare was "Da-dum, da-dum, da-dum, da-dee. Until we meet in Vic—tor—ree!" Massimo made Gloria laugh.

Gloria never lost an argument to a man. Her mind was too nimble, her words weighty and quick, prizefighters, every one of them. Men emerged dazed and wiser from mental battle with Ms. G. Arguing was one of Gloria's favorite games. Ideas were toys. Thoughts on their own were useless to her, they were to have fun with, and she'd just as soon not have any if there were no other minds about for playmates. She did not trust ideas any more than she trusted a baseball. Is it coming toward me or from me? How fast? How high? Low? An idea was a ball, but the game could be catch, could be dodge ball. What she trusted were feelings, both sensory and emotional. These were real to her, unfalse, unfaked. The smallness of a pebble or sea glass, a warm look's grip on a heart, the dry crack of broken twigs when livings played soccer at 102nd Street, these were immutable, dependable to always be what they were. Men were real to Gloria. As challenging as her intellect was, Gloria was a fool for men, and she felt lucky to have met one for whom she could be a fool without being foolish.

Robbie didn't know and Gloria didn't tell her. Gloria believed in her friendship. If anyone would have criticized Robbie, Gloria would have defended her. Although who would criticize Robbie? She was so sweet, so nice. She was beautiful, but didn't have the 'I'm so fine' attitude. Robbie had spent her whole life fighting her way into the background. She was really good at it. Wraiths who knew about Gloria and Massimo said Robbie was stupid. She wasn't stupid, just ignorant. There was compliance to keep her that way.

Compliance

The Same Summer

"I have a gift for portraiture," Bartalemeo Mio announced. His self-portrait was a masterpiece. Passers-by offered him money for it. A self-identified serious collector offered him twenty-five hundred. Bartalemeo Mio refused. "Not for sale." He made arrangements to show the collector his other work; the savvy woman bought a small pen and ink study of a child.

"You have a gift, a real gift for portraiture," she said.

By now Bartalemeo had developed a persona among the Sheep Meadow regulars. He was the handsome artist who talked to himself while he painted. Bartalemeo didn't know who he was talking to. An unknown someone had saved his life and he had no way to thank the person other than to live his life well and share how he was living it. There was a very simple explanation for what had happened with the emerald and diamond: Bartalemeo had a fairy godmother. Or godfather. Either way, Bartalemeo knew he was protected and cared for, and after knowing so well the feeling of not being protected and cared for, Bartalemeo Mio had to let his caring protector know he was grateful.

So he talked. But to who? Bartalemeo Mio looked at each stranger as potentially "the one." No one was too old or too ragged. In truth, he suspected the giver of the jewels was a crazed park bum who collected bottles for nickels and slept wrapped in newspaper. He looked at these people more kindly now, with greater interest, with recognition. The man in the blue pants with the blue beard and the shirts stuffed under his shirt was different from the woman with the too-big sneakers and the battered fedora. He painted the man in blue and drew songbirds around his head. That one sold quickly. The vacancy in the subject's eyes added to his saintliness. The man ran way, flinging curses over his shoulder when Bartalemeo Mio tried to give him the money from the sale.

"I would like to do your portrait," became the first thing Bartalemeo Mio said every morning when he set up to work. "What colors should I have? What brush is right for your eyebrows? Are you a man whose wife has died? No man wears rocks as big as the ones you gave me unless he is a king with a crown or a high religious figure. Are you a woman? I can't imagine I wouldn't have noticed a woman in the Ramble. No, you're a man. Definitely.

"Right?"

When Bartalemeo Mio moved to the carousel, he continued to talk while he worked, so sure was he that at least some of the time his fairy godfather was nearby. Could it be the little guy with the ponytail who ran the carousel? Bartalemeo Mio did his portrait, too, between two horses' heads. It came out colorful, the man more elfin than ever compared to the wooden horses with their dead gazes. The carousel operator wanted to buy that one; he paid more than he thought he would for it, and treasures it beyond the money he spent.

Throughout the bright and noisy summer children stayed away from the crazy artist.

"I'd like to do your portrait," Bartalemeo Mio said. "I imagine you are blond, and slim and slightly tall, and that your hair is longish." Ivan was surprised by the accuracy. "I think you are old. Very old. You are like a father to me; perhaps there is even some resemblance between us. Perhaps that is why you chose me. Perhaps you have a Roman nose like I do. Or stern eyebrows. Would I be right to paint you patrician, in a toga, or better to picture you in a t-shirt leaning against a pillar in the subway?"

Bartalemeo Mio lost belief that he would meet his benefactor but talking to him tore holes in the artist's imagination. Once a neat, symmetrical room, questions had poked through the floor and ceiling and walls of that part of his mind; dirt blew in and collected in piles and seeds settled in the piles and sprouted flowers. Every so often the young artist would make bouquets from the flowers to show he knew the holes were not there to hurt him.

"My life has a repeating pattern. It is this: start off with a bang, then fizzle. First day of school, my hand was always up, by winter holiday, the teacher had forgotten I was in the classroom. At parties, girls would flock to me when I walked in the room; by the last song I was in the kitchen by the sink, barely listening to a girl trying to make herself useful by washing the dishes. I'm afraid this portrait thing is the same. The spark is going. Maybe I'll refresh in Italy. Look at the Michelangelo's. His women look like men with breasts. I wouldn't paint women that way. Still, he is the master of the masters. Should I go? Do you want me to study in Europe?"

The very next day Ivan showed himself to Bartalemeo Mio. Never one to eschew drama, Ivan waited for his moment. He let Bartalemeo Mio set himself up at the center of the Terrace between the double grand staircase down to The Lake. It was a sparkling day. Cyclists speeding between east side and west. Pedestrians striding in time to their earphoned music. One of the Fauves followed two schoolgirls in plaid uniforms. He waved at Ivan. Ivan waved back, hoping the Fauve wouldn't stop. He didn't. When Bartalemeo's paints were laid out and the canvas on its stand and the water in its cup, starting at Bartalemeo Mio's feet, Ivan laid out his emeralds, diamonds, rubies and pearls in a trail like Hansel and Gretel's which Bartalemeo Mio followed, picking up the baubles (for in such abundance, they were more curiosities of prettiness than concentrated wealth), shoving them one by one into his increasingly misshapen pockets, all the way down the stairs, under the vaulting arches to the fountain, where Ivan positioned himself on the lip of the pool so Bartalemeo Mio would have to look up at him and see him framed by the angel and the sky. Then Ivan appeared to Bartalemeo Mio. Ivan later told Robbie, "I was nervous as a virgin."

"I want to paint you," Bartalemeo Mio said. He backed away from Ivan, then turned and ran up the stairs, looking anxiously back over his shoulder, stumbling. Ivan waited. He closed his eyes on the retreating figure of Bartalemeo Mio. His body was still, his mind was frantic. Please do not leave me. I'm the one you've been telling your stories to. I'm the one you've wanted to see. Here I am. He heard the paints and easel as Bartalemeo Mio banged down the stairs.

"What have I done to the boy?" Ivan wondered through his smile.

"So you'll sit for me? It'll take a while. Days, at least. You'll stay? I didn't know you'd look like this. I thought you'd be older. Fully dressed." He laughed. He was a little embarrassed by Ivan's near nakedness. He set up carefully.

"I was born in 1932," Ivan said. He waited for the confusion to get a good hold on Bartalemeo Mio's face.

"You're a runner?"

"I'm a ghost. When I was alive, I taught martial arts. Among other things. It's why my muscles are the way they are."

"I...can anyone else see you?"

"No. Nobody living."

"Why can I see you?"

"Because I let you." Better not to tell the boy the price of that decision. Unfair to have him share the weight of another's choice.

"Thank you." Bartalemeo Mio's hands moved quickly. "Why'd you choose me?"

Ivan shrugged and wondered if he were learning discretion.

More visitors were arriving at the Bethesda Fountain Plaza. There were many who stopped to watch Bartalemeo Mio work and puzzle over what he was painting. For there was the angel statue and the shimmer of water, and edging of trees, on the canvas as in the park. But on the canvas, just off center was also a man, muscular, fair-haired, bare-chested, with a medieval page's hairdo and remnants of what had been trousers. The details were so real, the shine in the man's hair, the droop of the waistband, the small glint of a gem in his earlobe, it was disconcerting to look away from the painting and find the man not there. Passersby knew they were in the presence of genius. The respectful ones moved away; the bold ones asked questions, the sophisticates asked for his card. Bartalemeo Mio treated them all the same, that is, he paid them no attention.

He had eyes and ears for only his subject, and he continued to talk to him. Why, when he had talked to a dream, would he stop when it came real?

"Either you are real, or I have lost my mind. I think if I were going to lose my mind I would have done it before now, no? When I couldn't paint? I could tell. I was trying, going through the motions, promising that practice was what I needed, but I knew I wasn't painting. I wasn't improving day by day or even month by month. I was getting worse. Do you know I threw all those canvases from last year away? They weren't even bad. Energy-less. When I'm famous, I don't want those things surfacing and spoiling my reputation. But enough about me. What do you think about me?" He shook his head and his laugh was the music his curls danced to.

Had a day ever been more beautiful? Had a reality ever exceeded a dream so fully? Had the drummers ever sounded so African? Had the midriffs of the girls with their blouses tied under their bosoms ever been so tight? Had the crowd ever been so milling, so merry? No, never.

"So tell me about yourself," Bartalemeo Mio said. He was nervous. Give him credit for speaking at all. For he did believe what Ivan told him. He accepted that Ivan was a dead man as surely as he accepted he had a pocketful of stones to keep him in apartment and paints for life. "I'm going to leave early today, before the sun goes down; I don't want to be in the park at dark with this fortune in my pocket. But tomorrow, we will talk all day, all night. As long as we want." Even so, after Bartalemeo Mio parted across the street from Cooper Hewitt, Ivan worried that he would never come back. What if he had frightened the boy so much that he never entered the park again? What if he packed up and moved to another city, what if he put oceans between them? What if Bartalemeo Mio didn't like him?

Ivan was just teasing himself.

"You know when somebody likes you," Robbie said. Together she and Ivan combed through the details like teenagers. What was the look on Bartalemeo Mio's face when Ivan showed himself? Was he blasé? Stunned? What did he say, exactly? How did he say what he said?

Of course Bartalemeo Mio came back. Early the next day, and a long parade of days after.

Robbie didn't show herself to Bartalemeo Mio, but she did watch. Robbie's friend and his great love were a good couple. But then, how could anyone not get along with Ivan?

Bartalemeo Mio was happy talking to Ivan. Day by day his artifice fell away and together the two of them grew lighter until their buoyant words floated about them in heart-shaped balloons. The portrait progressed.

"Don't paint me with a hard-on."

"I paint what I see."

"I don't want to make my entrance into art history with a hard-on."

"Then let's do something about it." Afternoons after observing Ivan and Bartalemeo Mio, Robbie was tenderer with Massimo. He was as tender as a nurse with her.

In Bartalemeo Mio's portrait of him, Ivan looked like a saint, floating, as he did, above the ground. Bartalemeo Mio got the hair just right, heavy, blond, shoulder-length. ("About the head I look like a Breck boy.") The muscles of his chest and arms had a Renaissance look to them. "Highly and wittily influenced by Michelangelo," said *Art and Antiques*. The painting caused quite a stir, not only because of its technical virtuosity, but because it was a picture, Bartalemeo Spano (this was his name) insisted, of a living dead man. Artists, we all know, are a little bit crazy. Some not so little bit. And the picture had a funny name, too. "Yvonne." Stories sprang up about who Yvonne was. A woman who left Spano for the saint in the picture. A woman who was dearly beloved, but a nun? One reporter went to the Catholic school Spano had attended as a child.

"He was a dear, dear child. Very special. Quiet." Sister Mary Margaret said. She had him confused in her mind with other children: the sister found all children dear and special because so they were in the eyes of her Lord; all the children in her classes were quiet, she beat the ones who weren't. What she was saying was he conformed like all the others. He learned his lessons; he didn't make himself stand out. Sister Mary Margaret was not a self-reflective woman. Else she would have wondered why she, like so many grown-ups, valued conformity in children and gave lip service at least, to non-conformity in adults. Difference made her uncomfortable; it didn't fit her scheme of what obedience meant. And yet, she was sincerely happy for the success of one of her former pupils, even if she wasn't entirely sure which one he had been, and she was pleased that the eager reporter was so attentive to her recollections. "He was very good at sketching." Here, the sister was stretching the truth to make the reporter happy. Drawing was, to Sister Mary Margaret's mind, a waste of time and not much of it happened in her classroom. She thanked God she hadn't thwarted the boy's natural gifts and admonished herself to give more time to crayons.

Many paintings of Ivan followed.

Ivan loved posing. The languid attitude in his face, the turn of his knee, the relaxedness in the paintings didn't match his own image of himself.

"Very come hither, isn't it?" Bartalemeo Mio agreed.

Robbie was waiting for Gloria at the Naturalists Gate. They'd been together less, what with Robbie's fascination with Ivan and Bartalemeo Mio, and Gloria's zero interest, but today they had a date for when the sun was at the left side of the Plaza Hotel. Robbie had taken to sitting on benches with her feet on the seat and her butt on the back, the way Gloria did. It felt free, masculine.

"Robbie. You are becoming so unlady-like." It was The Duchess, taking Winken, Blinken and Nod for a walk. She didn't seem to be any more saintly since she'd had her first dream, and then her second. Perhaps more independent as Seneca wasn't always in her entourage any longer.

"Hello, Duchess." Robbie had to admit that The Duchess looked radiant. Still the high, haughty chin. The fighting nose, the slightly protruding eyes. A dame. Was she ever a babe? Robbie doubted it. She pictured The Duchess in a high collar, a full skirt, her waist cinched in, her hair piled high above her head, maybe a bit of rouge on her lips. The Duchess was talking.

"There is no reason for jewelry to be simple and shy. An oxymoron, defeats the purpose. Shiny stones, precious stones exist to be showy. Showy is their raison d'être. Why would you select a wallflower stone? Why would you select a setting that keeps the stone a secret? It's stupid. Emeralds, sapphires, diamonds, rubies, they are to catch light, to sparkle from a woman's fingers, neck, ears, hair, wrists. It is patently ridiculous to wear a quiet piece of jewelry. It's an insult to the stone; it goes against its nature.

"Except when one is speaking of jewelry, flashy is a pejorative. Flashiness is jewelry's entire point. So long as it is of flawless quality, of course. Mine always was."

Robbie wondered where Gloria was. Were they supposed to meet? Often, Robbie was noticing, her mind wandered. She would find herself thinking of people she'd known, smiling at happy things she remembered until she remembered to shut that box and not think of it any more. Then she'd find herself further north or south or east or west from where she'd been, later in the conversation. Did she talk during these blackouts? She didn't know. She doubted it. Why should she get a word in edgewise with these guys? All of them wanting to unload their stories. She used to like to hear other people's stories. They were good material for her fiction. When had they started feeling redundant?

The Duchess had done the babies' hair in modified Mohawks. Molding their hair up from the roots to the tips with mud with her handprints dried in it. The babies' bodies were covered with mud in Ndebele patterns, much of it smeared or flaked off, but enough still in evidence for the effect to be clear. The Duchess herself was marked with mud handprints about her shoulders and her thighs. The babies had fat thighs, rolls like donuts above their knees, their hands still pudgy. One baby taxied into the Duchess' lap, shoving her arm out of the way. He stood up on her thighs, grabbing, whenever he felt he might lose his balance, for anything in the direction of her head and although she twisted her face away from his open fist, she was at his disposal. He slid his sweet mud–painted arms around the Duchess's neck, his little finger-painted heinie facing Robbie.

"Do you think he'd let me hold him?" Robbie reached out for the baby. He shrank away from her, his face a mixture of fear and defiance. The Duchess shrugged. What could she do, except insist? And why should she?

The Duchess was still disturbing to Robbie. She wasn't coy about her nakedness. She was blatantly naked. Disapproving. Victorian in her expression and clearly focused on getting just what she wanted. There was a lot to admire in the Duchess. Her pride. One thing you had to say for her: she did not let go of who she was to be popular.

"They say I should've been a man. My father often said I was the son he never had. The difference of course was I could wrap my father around my little finger the way a son never could. My father took advantage of me as a young girl, and I learned to take advantage of him. Poor us."

"If I were a mother," said Gloria, slipping into the flow, "I'd be a Diva Mom. Like, I'd be the mother in the hat and the heels reading the principal. If I had a child, I'd change my drag completely and go Alexis on you all."

"The wonderful thing about becoming a mother is you can no longer put off being a person you admire," Robbie said. She was learning from Gloria, or from her anger at Gloria, not to submerge her own thoughts for the sake of letting others speak. Gloria's hogging the spotlight made Robbie face how much she wanted it herself. Courtesy begins at home. So Robbie kept talking, respecting what she herself had to say.

"In that way, I wasn't a good mother. I fed my child. I kept her in clean diapers and sang to her, and loved her more than life, but once you become a mother, you must live the life you want for your child. Do you want your child to travel across Europe and stay in nice hotels? Then you must travel across Europe and stay in nice hotels. If you want her to live in a house with fine things, then you must live with fine things. Do you want her to feel at home in countries around the world? Then you must live a month or two in Milano. A summer in Dakar. A winter in Jamaica.

"Do you want your child to feel physically secure? Then you must take karate lessons. Children do what you show them. So you must become what you want your child to be. Whatever your fantasy for your child, you must live yourself."

"She's right, you know," The Duchess said and rolled off, trailing her triplets.

"I think there's a storyteller at the Discovery Center. Want to go there and listen to some stories?" Gloria said.

Robbie liked the looks of the Discovery Center. It was a fairy-tale cottage at the top of the park on the edge of a pond. Gloria and Robbie sat in an open window while Malika Lee Whitney told tales in a voice spiked with the flavors of the Caribbean.

Afterwards, Gloria and Robbie glinded together around the park like invisible fish in a bowl, mostly quiet between them. Gloria offered to twist Robbie's dreads, the sensation of which, the pulling and stretching and kneading of scalp, was the most pleasurable in the world for Robbie. The women sat on a bench down by Central Park South, across from a tower that told the time. They were near a statue of a man on a horse. No one had died knowing the rider's name, and, of course, it was too late to read it. Gloria sat on the bench back and Robbie rested between her knees.

Gloria said, "You know, 'I'm learning a lot,' is Black Girl code for 'Things aren't easy right now. I'm struggling. When I get through this – and I will get through this – I'll be a stronger person. Because what doesn't kill you makes you stronger and I refuse to let this kill me.' That's what it means when you ask a woman how it's going and she answers that she's learning a lot." Gloria massaged Robbie's head. Robbie squeezed her eyes shut and sank into the sensation. Gloria was saying, "When someone says, 'I'm learning a lot,' that's your cue to stand on the sidelines and cheer, 'You go, Girl!' You make a chant of it. 'You go, Girl. You go, Girl. Girlfriend. Girlfriend."

Gloria patted her foot.

"You go, Girl.

(Snap finger.)

You go, Girl.

(Snap finger.)

Girlfriend.

(Stomp, stomp.)

Girlfriend.

(Stomp, stomp.)

She played with that awhile.

"You go, Girl. (and three, four)

You go, Girl. (and three, four)

Girlfriend. (and four)

Girlfriend." (and four)

Gloria worked into a nice groove. Robbie felt Gloria's strong fingers at her scalp. The gentle pulsing of Gloria's calf muscles against her arm as Gloria pumped her foot in the rhythm. Robbie remembered the times she had stood on the sidelines cheering, "You go, Girl."

Cecelia, who married at sixteen, three months after her father died. After many years, after her youngest child married and had a child of her own,

Cecelia left her marriage. She went into divorce, her own apartment, pierced ears, short hair, and a date with a man from the personals ads in the back the New York Times Book Review whom she marries happily ever after. After a marriage to please her dead father, she made one to please herself. You go, Girl.

Althea, who cut her paying job down to two days a week so she could start a new career as an actor. You go, Girl.

Samantha, who mortgaged her home to start her business and slept on the couch for four years because what used to be her bedroom held three desks, three computers and four phones. Her children slept with her. She built a tent around the couch to make it fun for everybody. Yes to signing the lease on commercial space, yes, to the bank that believed in you enough to put money on the line. Yes. You go, Girl.

Angela went off the deep end when her ridiculously wealthy husband left her by surprise and quite publicly for a Brazilian playgirl. Angela lay in bed letting the phone ring while her cheerleaders left messages, "How are you?" "I love you." "Are you okay?" "If I don't see you out there running tomorrow, I'm going to break in and snatch you out of there." The only thing Angela did was get her kids dressed and out the door to their driver every morning in time for school. She didn't eat, she didn't bathe, she didn't want to live. All she wanted was to love her children. That was the rope hanging down the well she was in. That's the rope she climbed up and out of the well on, hands bruised, legs rope burned. She became a funny, involved mother, not just to her own kids, but to the kids on the block, and in her children's teams, and the children at the foundling hospital and their teenage mothers. You go, Girl.

Ghillie who sued her ex-employer for firing her unfairly. She faced all the questions and lies about her competence, her commitment, and her attitude and came out whole. Girl! You go.

Robbie remembered the times people stood on the sidelines for her. So many times. When she'd lost her job and her husband wasn't working. When she failed to get a grant she'd worked hard on. The week between her biopsy and the report. They'd been there, "You go, Girl."

Gloria patted the back of Robbie's head, then pushed her forward and swung her own leg over Robbie's head, and slid down to sit next to Robbie.

"You should know I'm seeing Massimo," she said.

No. No. Robbie shook her head, but even while she denied it, she knew it was true, and the knowing made her rock, made her whole body shake up and down. Yes. Her arms around her chest, her head between her elbows, she banged her back against the bench so hard it seemed she might go through it, and she let out noises, too, that she didn't know she had. Her body rocked yes, and her head shook no, and the noises that she made rose like atom bombs. Rorschach tests of sound. Her hard eyes squeezed out tears she thought she didn't have, that came with the rocking and shaking.

Gloria sat beside her silent, not crying, listening. Gloria was there heavy and accepting, until Robbie threw her hand in the air and waved her away.

How could Gloria explain?

"I'm in love with Gloria." Massimo told Robbie. When he said it, he held Robbie's hand and would not let her wrestle it free. Surely it was like a coal in his hand, her whole body was fire. Her heart was a furnace, her face its open door. Weren't her dreadlocks flames bursting and consuming about her? If he didn't let go of her hand, he would burn, too. All that would be left of him, cinders.

When Robbie was alive, she wanted to hit the men who'd broken up with her. They did it for her own good, always because they "didn't deserve" her. At least Massimo wasn't lying. He loved Gloria. Gloria? Gloria wasn't his type. She was sloppy. She was careless. She said stuff she didn't mean just to see the kind of trouble it'd cause. She was drugged as often as she had the chance.

"I wish I wasn't hurting you," Massimo said. "I'd do anything not to hurt you."

"Gloria?"

"You love her, too." He laughed. Robbie did hit him. "She suggested I not stop seeing you. She thought it would be wisest to share."

"How generous. Why'd you say no? Or are you saying yes?"

"I'm saying no."

"So am I." They were bouncing on the balls of their feet, sparring partners. Not wanting to hurt, but wanting to win. Old jagged feelings for weapons, more bark than bite.

"She lets me love her. She enjoys my love. She isn't afraid for me to see the parts I might not approve of. And then, when she lets me see them, it's like they're not faults anymore. I'm like an antibiotic to all her viruses. She trusts me to love her. I know she'd just as soon tell a tale as the truth. I know she'll blow off a whole week, easy. While you and I, you and I will make something useful to do."

"She doesn't deserve your love."

'What's deserve got to do with it? I know you deserve my love. You look right, you act right, and you follow all the rules that surround me. Robbie, I love you. I do."

"You just love Gloria more."

"If you wish."

"I don't wish. I don't wish. Gloria creates drama. All her adjectives have roots in four-letter words. Gloria is cheap."

Those are not the things one says (even if one thinks them) about a friend. A friend doesn't take your boyfriend, either.

"This is the first time I ever fought for a man not to leave me. I'm not too good at it. I should have a least held on to my pride. See ya." She glinded away.

"I love you, Robbie," he called.

"Whatever gets you through the night."

"We both love you."

"Fuck you, asshole."

The night of Gloria and Massimo's and The Duchess and the Triplets' non voyage, Robbie ran into Seneca not far from the theatre.

"You're not going to the party?" Robbie said. Seneca shook her head. She sat in a tree that Robbie had seen her in before, many times. Right off the road near 82nd Street. Robbie leapt up to a lower branch. After all this time, she still liked the feeling of sitting on a branch, legs dangling in space. It felt dangerous. "You've been here a long time, too."

Seneca nodded. Her skin was very dark and very clear. Her eyes, too. "'I shouldn't have said that." Robbie said. She was right. It was like asking someone her age. Worse.

"I can go to Heaven when I give up my right to be angry." She stared ahead. It was a beautiful night. Stars shot across the sky. "I don't want to give it up."

Robbie heard that Gloria and Massimo's and The Duchess-with- triplets' non-voyage party was the best in anyone's memory. It was the first time the Fauves came to a non-voyage. A few wraiths swore that angels came down from Heaven too, wearing spandex pants with legwarmers and platform shoes and tube tops and iridescent shirts with big collars. They were reported to have shimmered, like oversized Tinkerbells, but they sweated, too. At first the wraiths kept their distance, but then one of the Fauves taught one of angels the Electric Slide and the rest was, as they say . . . Massimo had shaved his beard. His face looked silly, and he didn't care. Women kissed his tiny little heart-shaped chin, the chin that he hated. Overheard between dances:

"You were too perfect before."

"Huh?"

"Chinks in the armor let me in. Anyway, who said your little chinny chin chin was a fault?"

Robbie was told this, against her will, and walking away, waved her hand, languidly, negligently, a kind of Peter O'Toole gesture.

Gloria gave a performance at the celebration. Here's what she said: "God is good. I want you to understand what I'm saying when I say that. God is good. I don't mean 'good' as in 'wouldn't hurt a fly.' God's goodness is good as in 'Damn, I'm good.' God does what She does well. God works it."

Robbie knew why Massimo preferred Gloria. Gloria was who she was. Robbie was just pretending. When Gloria loved, it was true love. Gloria had honored

Massimo with her love, her true love, which was the only kind she could give. Robbie couldn't give true love because she couldn't be true. Hadn't she filtered herself through "what does he want?" every time she presented herself to him? Did she love Massimo wholly? She couldn't say she had. She thought he was right for her. Her love was a showroom model love. Rehearsed and rehashed. Gloria's love was live.

Fall
Winter
Early Spring

If there were any doubts about Bartalemeo Mio's depth as an artist, any suspicions that he was a mere flavor of the month and not a talent for the ages, they fell like the walls of Jericho to the shout of his winter series. Critics saw the paintings as direct descendant in the Hudson River School; urban pastorals. "...soft shades of white, all the colors of snow, its bright sparkles and quiet shadows... Restful and still." (*Art and Antiques*) Some made fun of them, those that did not see them in person, but only the reproductions in magazines. People who cared enough to actually have a face-to-face were awed.

In person, the entire series and the paintings individually had strength. One felt the chill of the air and the warm comfort of the snow, the inviting blanket of peace if one could just lie down in the snow. A blanket of lightness and warmth, and silence so serene it was like a chant. They were paintings in which your mind could make a home. The trees you were looking at became your trees, you knew them and grew them. Those mounds of snow were your mounds of snow, you could trace their contours in your sleep. The playground was your playground, holding the memories of your play. And the guests were your guests. Guests? Yes. If you looked long enough to make a home within the frame, you began to see your visitors. And soon the visitors took over the paintings like strong personalities in a beautiful room. Funny you didn't notice them before, and not all in the shadows, although some were. Others were in the sunlight, laughing, whispering to each other. They were magical. You felt not in the presence of genius, but the presence of love. Calm and joyful and secure. Gallery browsers girded themselves tight in their coats to avoid the invitation of snow when they walked out into the street.

How Bartalemeo Mio suffered for those ten paintings. His fingers were cold. "Go home. Drink chocolate. Hold your fingers between your thighs and warm them." Ivan would tell him.

"I can hold my fingers between my thighs and warm them here," Bartalemeo Mio answered. When he did go home tears flooded his eyes from the pain of his hands thawing.

"You can't come in weather like this. If you do, I won't meet you."

"I will."

"You can't come in weather like this."

"Says who?" Bartalemeo Mio smiled. Because he knew if he came, Ivan would be there, that Ivan could not stay away from him. He knew as well that he did not want to stay away from Ivan, who was so fascinating and patient and adoring and handsome. He nearly shone with beauty.

Ivan didn't talk about the other wraiths. He talked about himself as a living man, and as a dead one, but not about the other deads. Still, Bartalemeo Mio was an imaginative soul, how could he not be? He extrapolated other wraiths, in part because he did not want to imagine Ivan lonely. It was these extrapolations that he smuggled into his landscapes for the true appreciators to see.

Bartalemeo Mio started talking about committing suicide in the park so that he could die and be with Ivan. First he posited it as a question, what would happen if? Ivan laughed and almost wove a high color story about endless nights of petting and parties, a story with broad strands of Robin Hood and Peter Pan, but he thought better of it.

"That wouldn't be good," he said.

"But I just want to know what would happen if I came to the park one day, finished my final masterpiece and committed hari kari. Maybe that's a painting I could do first. First I'll paint myself doing hari kari, then I'll pull out a sword and disembowel."

"That's disgusting."

"I bet it would cement my place in art history." Bartalemeo Mio had the future planned. Not just his future, the future.

"As a loony. It's a horrible idea and I am not amused."

'What do you think? That I'll grow older and you'll stay young? Forget about it."

Ivan didn't talk about it but he didn't forget about it either. When Bartalemeo Mio brought it up again, Ivan let his anger show. The third time, Ivan let his fear show, which Bartalemeo Mio interpreted as love. And it was true that Ivan did love the painter, not only his beautiful face and body, but his wit and talent and kindness and desire to be good.

"If you entertain this suicide idea one more time, I will leave you. Please, please don't ever think of it again. I will love you forever. Alive, dead, it doesn't make any difference. You see?" The next time Bartalemeo Mio played with the idea Ivan said, "One more time, and I'm outta here. I'm not playing." Bartalemeo Mio believed him. But the idea stuck and the boy grew fonder and fonder of it. He was convinced that he could convince Ivan. "We spend so much time together. Wouldn't it make more sense for me to just go ahead and move in?"

"You will never find me again." Ivan disappeared right in front of Bartalemeo Mio's eyes.

Ivan stopped talking. Robbie recognized it first; many other wraiths had given him wide berth ever since he gave The Duchess' emerald away. They are, however, a loyal community, and seeing him alone they no longer shunned him. They tried to draw him into conversation. Then they worried about him. And then slowly, they came to him to talk. Sometimes it was as if he wasn't listening, but at least he could be depended on not to interrupt. He sat, thinking perhaps, at the edge of the boat dock after it closed for the evening.

"Ivan, how you doin'? Long time, no see, Man. Where you bean, Chilly? Rodriguez told me he seen you, Man, over up by the Police Station. What you doing, checking out the cops changing into they uniforms? They got some nice looking guys there, huh? Not that I got anything against looking at them, I do that my damn self. One of those guys, I saw him go from skinny new guy, he used to work out with his t-shirt on, with the weights they got in there? Then he got fat, retired. I saw his whole career, Man. I been here all that time, Man. You been here longer than me." Ivan didn't even know who said this to him, some guy; he barely paid attention.

Robbie was hurt that he wouldn't talk to her. She was his favorite. He was special to her. Still, even while she resented his silence, she respected it. He'd said, it seemed, all he had to say. Then he shut up. That'd been one of Robbie's problems. The gift of gab but not the gift of shut up. She always had to remake her point, and for what?

Once Exo joined Ivan in Hans Christian Andersen's lap. Ivan looked at him, then turned back to the model boats on the Conservatory Water.

"Ivan. I been thinking, I been thinking, that I want to get this gap in my leg closed. People don't like to look at me. I used to not care. I don't like scaring people any more. I used to get off on it, you know? Now, it's a drag."

In the Shakespeare Garden, colorless this time of year: "Ivan. What's going to happen if you keep yourself isolated like this? You'll lose your mind, my friend."

Among Alice in Wonderland's animals: "Are you Ivan? They told me I'd recognize you."

Robbie took to sitting next to Ivan. At first she scared away the people who came to talk. In time they got used to her, they accepted her as an adjunct the way livings accept pets with their owners. They came and talked to Ivan.

At the opera: "I had my dream. It was of my mother. She was floating towards me on a rubber mattress, the kind you see in pools. Naw, Man. I made that up. I'll just sit here a minute. Okay?

"See you later. Thanks."

"Ivan. I saw some people dressed all in white kill twelve chickens up at the North Meadow. They had dancers and drummers, the rhythm was unbelievable. Bap bah-dah bah-dah bah-dah bah-dah bap! And then they had this other brother jump in. One-a. One-a, one-a, one-a, one-a. Then this other brother came in, and this sister, her fingers were going so fast I couldn't even seen them, by the time I got to focus on where they were they were somewhere else and gone.

"It was wild. Women dancing and speaking in tongues. Everybody was hugging himself or herself and bowing to each other. There were spirits there; a lot of them, the meadow was crowded with spirits. Like it was a concert for spirits. For all I know, it might have been. I couldn't see them, but you could feel it for real. The spirits were partying and arguing and drinking and eating like livings, but I couldn't see them. Next time, I'm going to find you and bring you up there."

Robbie never watched who was speaking, never looked in the direction of the speaker. She let their lives rinse through her; they touched her without noticing her. There was comfort, even happiness.

Summer
Winter
Spring
Fall
Summer
Winter

Exo dropped down beside Robbie at the skating rink downtown. He didn't usually come so far south. He was wearing a wispy van Dyke beard, in the way of the Fauves, now, in honor of Massimo and his pointy little chin. Down the road to Fifth Avenue, a tall woman, sturdy and black, yelled, "In hell, there is no amnesia."

"You can sew, right?" Exo asked.

"Yeah. Some." Robbie said.

"Like you could sew a hole in a sock, right, or if I like ripped a seam in my jeans, right?"

"Yeah."

"Could you sew up my leg?" Exo said. Down Exo's front thigh and around to the back of his knee and into the top of his knotty calf stretched a rip. "I got caught over a razor wire." Strips of fabric held in his innards, string, whatever he could piece together to make a length long enough to wrap and tie around his leg. The wound was not active, but it was raw. Over the years Robbie had learned not to look. And now he wanted her to touch it? Yuck. Her own scrape had gotten dirty and flakes had scaled off over the years, but the skin was not torn deeply and nothing inside showed. "I have needle and thread," Exo said. Gifts from the living world had started showing up by the wraiths that needed them. A sewing kit from a hotel had been in Exo's hand when he climbed out of his hole this morning. Strange.

Robbie sewed. She didn't know whether it hurt or not; she didn't ask. Once, her needle jabbing through a tough scar, she looked at Exo's face. His eyes were closed, his lips whistled silently. The rest of the time she concentrated on the job at hand. She stuffed his muscles and vessels in close to the bones. Exo gripped the torn skin and Robbie blanket-stitched the edges together. She learned as she went along, in increasingly non-skin-toned thread. She got a feel for what was too tight and made the skin stretch, what was too close together so the skin tore more. By the time she got down to the knee she was confident enough and focused enough to knot a springy tendon to a bone, jamming the needle into the top of the tough strip and wrapping the other end of the green thread through a hole in the bone. Exo stood and walked on it a few steps. He limped less. Exo pulled his shin skin together and she went back to sewing.

The hardest part was the calf. Small as his legs were, bandy as the calves were, the skin didn't want to reach all the way around. They finally decided on sewing twice, zigging on the first pass and zagging on the second. When they were done the stitches across the back of Exo's leg were crossed coyly, like the bodice of a scullery maid's corset. Peeking out provocatively, not the sweet swell of young breasts, but barely restrained flesh, all the same.

"Kind of sexy," Robbie pronounced it.

“Thanks,” Exo said. “Thanks a lot, man.”

Another Winter Ends

The wind was fierce. The wraiths covered their eyes and clamped their mouths against it to move. And move they had to because the wind whipped around, searching, it seemed, for directions to go in order to hit them straight in their faces. A day in which it was easy to believe that everything had a spirit, most of which were evil. A day in which it was hard not to believe that all happens with intention. The wind spiraled around trees after the wraiths, ran ambushes around the Swedish Cottage, The Dairy, the Carousel, the pavilions around the lake. It pelted the Fortress with pebbles and ran all the Fauves southward.

Grit ground into everyone's eyeballs, dead leaves and bits of bark flew into their mouths. The wind snatched and tossed everything that wasn't nailed down. It even smashed wraiths against the barrier outside which they could not go. If you tried to walk into the park that day and it was especially hard, it might have been just the wind, or you might have been battling the wind and walking through a wraith. That is hard for livings, agony for wraiths, but possible.

"Where can we go?" Nearly everyone ended up in the hollow of the East Meadow, away from buildings being better than next to them. The only place that felt even a little safe was behind another wraith. Robbie thought perhaps they could protect each other. If some were barriers, the others could be safe. She thought it could work if she stepped out and spoke the idea. If she stepped out and spoke her idea she might be ridiculed. Who would want to suffer so someone else could have relief? Who would listen to her?

"I have an idea," Robbie said.

"What?" Where was the voice coming from? Robbie couldn't tell. The wind was grabbing words and throwing them around.

"I have an idea. Let's make two circles."

"Huh?"

"Two circles. One inside the other." She waved her arms, demonstrating, yelling what to do, and pulling wraiths into place in two concentric circles. All the wraiths in the outside circles faced inwards, shoulder to shoulder, arms around each other's waists, moving clockwise looking forward to their time to be inside. Inside circle wasn't wind-free, but much better. It was sweetest inside the circle the first few moments after being outside. The ones on the inside circle weren't totally protected, but enough that they could rest, wipe their eyes and breathe. Someone figured out that with a smaller circle some could be in the center, and that worked best of all.

Days later Robbie heard wraiths bragging about their parts.

"How many times were you out, man?" one wraith said to another.

"I did four tours without a break."

"You lyin'!"

"No. Four, back-to-back."

"Damn, the most I did in a row was two. But I did about fifteen tours in all."

"For real? That wind whipped my ass. Once I got inside I stayed inside. I saw niggas I ain't seen in years! It was like being at the Penn Relays. Don't laugh, man."

"Naw. I know what you mean. I gotta hand it to Robbie. That was a good idea she had."

"Robbie. I always thought she was stuck up. That sister's heavy."

Robbie and Exo were sitting at Summit Rock, the highest natural point in Central Park. Seneca had played there long before there was a Central Park.

Robbie said, "It seemed like a lot of wraiths were in the circles. It got me wondering. Does anybody know how many there are here? And then, I was thinking, is it possible to know? Is there ever anyone who just wakes up here and then they're gone, right away? Any people who died at the moment when all was right with them for going to Heaven? A bike messenger gets hit, body slams a couple of you Fauves, then gets sucked into Heaven. 'Cool. See ya!' Do you think that happens?"

"Sure it happens. You hear about those things secondhand. There're stories like that," Exo said.

Spring Back

The wraiths were back on their glass beach on the roof above the American Wing, baking face up, then face down, dancing to the music from the cyclists taking their boom boxes for a ride up the drive. Morning came early, the sun left late and all day in between was a party. Gossip. Stories of what happened over the winter. Snippet of conversation from the west side of the roof: “Rodrigo had his party. You didn’t know? It was hot. Some of everything was there. Nobody gave him a damn thing to take up to Heaven, though. That boy’s a thief to his heart. I would have given him something to take to my mother for me, only I don’t have spit.”

Snippet of a story from mid-roof: “Michael snuck into the museum and got locked in. He was liking it for a little while; he sat on the armored horsemen’s horses, he slid down banisters, felt up the statues. But then his fear of the dark from when he was a living snuck up on him and the next time the doors were opened, he got the hell out of there. I’d hate to be locked in a museum. Too much stuff that can come alive and get you.”

Another bit: “Ivan never had his dreams. That whole thing was a way to get The Duchess to pay him what she owed him . . . No, he didn't tell me that. I'm just putting two and two together."

Robbie overheard that and found it offensive. What kind of story was that? Much better narrative if Ivan had his dream, at least the first one, and gave up Heaven for love. It felt almost like an even trade – until the love was lost, like Ivan was lost to her. Every once in a while she thought she might have seen him. Sometimes she'd think he was nearby. But actual sightings were rare, and reports were suspect.

"Want to play unwrap the good times?" Exo asked. Robbie looked at him with surprise. "We spied on you and Ivan," he said. "You've got a good time all tied up back there. Let's hear it." He tapped her foot with his toe like Ivan used to do when they went out in a boat.

"It was grass the color of The Duchess' hair. Not quite red, brighter than brown." Already Exo was smiling. It was a good day to hear a good time.

"I'm sitting on Andy's couch, cleaning an ounce. Shaking out the seeds, picking out the twigs."

"Cleaning an ounce?"

"I was new to pot smoking then, and anal. Andy has a penthouse apartment on East 78th Street. His aunt owns the apartment, his family is wealthy. I have no numbers to attach to that, but his mother has an original Gauguin – a big one – in the family living room. Andy's a doctor, very good looking. His brothers are a lawyer, a student, a developer. One's collecting oral histories of war in South America. The cool one."

"I don't want the whole love affair, just a moment," Exo said.

"Okay. I'm sitting on his couch. The couch faces away from the study, through which one has to pass to reach the bedroom. I've never been to the bedroom, but it's visible through the study. To the left is a terrace that wraps around the apartment. New York is twinkling outside. We're reading. Prufrock. Seriously. I'd bought *The Golden Bough* for Andy for Christmas."

Robbie wondered if Exo knew what she was talking about. She doubted it. What did rich mean? Did he have any images attached to the name Gauguin? Did he know any poetry? She didn't remember much. "I grow old. I grow old. I shall wear the bottoms of my trousers rolled. I have heard the mermaids singing each to each. I do not think that they will sing to me." That was about it.

Robbie went on. "I'm pretending I'm comfortable in his place, but I'm not, really. There's a doorman downstairs who I figure knows who else is spending time with Andy and I'm always a little embarrassed when he greets me.

"I'm making this not a good memory, aren't I?

"Andy's at the bookcase behind the couch, looking up a word in the dictionary. He's disciplined about things like that. He's wearing the trousers to a suit and a light blue shirt and a tie. Everything he wears is subtle. Beautiful up close.

"I'm liking that a rich, handsome suit-wearing guy and I are reading poetry after a night at the theatre. And there's all this sexual tension between us because he's rich and I'm cool and he's white and I'm Black and we haven't done the dirty deed. I finish rolling a joint – it's something I'm good at – and I light it up and turn around to hand it to Andy. He replaces the dictionary and places the tips of his fingers on the back of my hand. 'I'd like you to spend the night.' I can still summon up the tingling that went through me with his fingertips on the back of my hand."

"That was good." Exo said. "Want to hear one of mine?

"My moms was very religious. Church ever Sunday and she didn't allow liquor in the crib."

(Exo falsettoed): " 'What if Pastor comes to our house and sees whiskey on my shelves?'

"So me and Moms had a problem. At first she didn't know I was drinking 'cause I kept it away from the house, but once I had a little money and could buy my own Jack Daniels, I got a bottle and I put it in a kitchen cabinet, high up where Moms couldn't see it.

"Well, what did I do that for? (Exo falsettoed again): "I found your friend Jack." I'm going to the shelf in the kitchen when she yells, 'I threw it down the drain.'

"So I, being no dummy, started hiding my whiskey in my closet where nobody can find nothing. And my moms, being sneaky, searched through my shit. One day I come home and she says, 'I'm so glad you stopped hanging out with your friend Jack.' I'm feeling smart for maybe a second until I process what Mom's saying: 'But you know the landlord doesn't let us keep pets.' That's how I knew she got rid of my Wild Turkey. I couldn't even be mad. Moms was funny."

Robbie tracked Ivan down at the edge of the Pond near 103rd Street, down under the overpass. Ducklings paraded behind their mother. Maybe the family scene gave Ivan some comfort or joy. Robbie couldn't tell. As for herself, Robbie felt uneasy there. The air by the pond was heavy on her. Ivan sat on a rock in a small peninsula into the water. Robbie squatted beside him. "Ivan, can I talk with you?"

Ivan stared at the ducks.

"I've been thinking about my house. The one I never bought? I spent years of weekends looking. I had a master plan, you know, with tile floors and stone walls and storage and no overhead kitchen cabinets and a back wall that rose up like a garage door. I could have made that home, too. But I didn't want to let go of the money and I let my little dreams relax under the weight of my even smaller reality. I wish I'd gone ahead and spent the money. I wish I had enjoyed the house. No, that's not right. I did enjoy the house, planning it in my mind. I wish I'd shared it. I wish I'd made it real for other people and shared it.

"I know what my sin is, was. I chose too small a life. But what can I do? Now? Choose a bigger life?"

Ivan winked at her.

Release

More and more, Robbie stayed in the Conservatory Garden. Its orderliness was restful to her. She had always been an identifier of patterns, an imposer of logic. Unless she could get a reasonable explanation for even unreasonable events, she was unsatisfied. The gardens were controlled. The paths were straight, the walkways were broad, the gardeners were friendly with visitors who talked about gardening. It was quiet. Robbie was lonely without Gloria and Massimo. Ivan was lost to her. Perhaps someday he would process all he'd been through and make a pronouncement. "And the answer is ---." And what would he say? Talking to Ivan was like talking down a deep well. His silence underlined her loneliness. Was it true that Heaven is the state of awareness that we are all God? How would that work? Robbie was speculating about Heaven more than she used to. Like Don Corleone enjoying wine more than he used to. She wandered to the center garden.

All the time she was spending here, the last time she'd spread out on the grass in the center garden was with Gloria. Wedding parties were still flowing through the gates and down the steps in extravagances of fabric. And between, people taking a stroll. Down the steps came a girl with Robbie's younger face.

Paloma.

Recognition struck Robbie's chest like an iron fist. Daughter. The girl was with a young man. They were talking. Robbie knew that her daughter would see her and recognize her. Robbie was on the verge of getting her life back, if that old story about Tre and his dog were true. It was delicious being on the edge where nothing would ever be the same and everything would always be better. All she had to do was glind over to the girl.

Robbie hid. Peeping from behind a bush she took in how her daughter looked. How her laugh sounded. Robbie remembered how she used to bounce Paloma on the bed to make her laugh. She's beautiful. More beautiful than I would have imaged when her face was round and multi-chinned. A lovely, long face with wide green eyes, eyebrows a little red at the inside corners, like they were when she was a baby. When she cried, they were angry spots in her face. My darling girl. She turned out nice. And what is that scar under her eye, faint, so faint, only a mother would see it? What happened to her to leave a scar? Did she fall? Was she hit? Did she cry, scared and in pain? Her mother wasn't there to hold her when it happened. And see, it all came out the same, just the same.

Her daughter. Unmistakably, yes. Robbie's husband's face, and her own, both together, then separate, at the turn of the child's head. Her fuzzy hair gathered light around her face. Her jeans had holes at the knees, very teen. Robbie wanted to tell Ivan. "Look at the child. My child. Was a smile ever sunnier? Listen to her. Was a wit ever quicker? Hear the bossiness in her tone? The child was born to rule." Since Ivan wasn't there, she crowed to herself. "My child." Of course, when she'd been alive, she wouldn't have confessed any of that. "All babies are cute," she'd replied to compliments on the baby's beauty. But she knew her child was exceptional. Her child was major gorgeous: even as a toddler people had turned on the street to watch her child. Does every Mother feel the same?

Paloma's young man was presentable except for the embarrassed little goatee. They chose a bench under apple trees heavy with blossoms. The little light that came through sparkled on the children's young faces. Paloma still had her constellation of dimples around her mouth. They danced when she talked. Both had clear skin, shining eye whites. Robbie stood behind the bench and eavesdropped. Then Paloma did the oddest thing. She turned around. Twisted her torso and looked straight at Robbie. And she said, "You're my mother."

And with those words, the boy could see Robbie, too. He boy put his arm around the girl and pulled her towards him. Silently, Robbie wished him away, to no effect at all. Protective skinny boy.

Now what? What did Robbie remember of the story of Tre leaving the park with his dog? Only that the dog had led him out. She didn't know for sure that Tre had rejoined life or continued as a ghost. She'd suspected the former, but then, she would. It was what she wanted. The young man complicated things. Robbie's emotions washed cares about him completely away when Paloma spoke.

"What's happening? I can't believe this." Paloma said. But she wanted her mother. Always in her life since her mother died, she had wanted her mother. Sometimes she wanted to yell at her mother, other times, just to talk, sometimes be kissed by and be quiet with. All her life she had been catching her breath at glimpses of women who might have been her mother, women with big smiles and good smells and pretty clothes.

"Those were my boots," Robbie said. All three of them looked at Paloma's boots, which had been Robbie's. When Robbie bought them, they were bright blue. They were no longer bright, no longer stiff and aggressive, but loved and oft-repaired and good with the torn jeans. Her girl had style.

"Have you been here the whole time?"

All those years. Why didn't you come see me? Why didn't you whisper to me when I was sad and tell me stories in the dark? Why did you stay here instead of being a mother to me? Roberta felt her daughter's hurricane of unsaid questions.

"I was here the whole time. Ever since I was dead I was stuck here. I couldn't leave. But I can leave with someone who loves me no matter what, and I love back the same way."

"Someone like me?" Paloma said.

"You're the only someone I've got."

"Would you like to come to my house?" Paloma said. Where did her fearlessness come from? Roberta thanked whoever had given it to her.

"I'll go with you," the boy said, grasping Paloma tighter.

"My name is Roberta Williams," Robbie said to the boy. She stuck her hand out for a shake. Next to the boy's hand hers was cracked and dirty, the nails broken and rough, the cuticles black even in the rips. The boy's hand was knobby with joints, large and clean. And so soft when he grasped hers. Did he really think he could protect Paloma with those soft hands? Did he really think he needed to? Robbie thought about her visual and admired the boy's restraint. And found him annoying in the extreme.

"Oh, I'm sorry," Paloma said. "You've heard of my mother. This is Ted." And so they all climbed the stairs to Fifth Avenue and 105th Street and walked downtown. Two teenagers and an apparent bag lady. If you noticed them at all, it would have been the long-legged girl you looked at. The woman with her was not as tall as she, but you could see the resemblance when they smiled the same big-toothed smile. If you paid attention, you might have noticed that the boy seemed superfluous, the way men can sometimes be in the company of women who are important to each other.

Outside the park wall was noisy; the din of traffic was painful to Roberta. And so crowded. It had been a long time since she'd stopped at a red light. Quaint. Walking was hard work. She'd forgotten how, how awkward the shifting of weight, the complications just to go from here to there. When she'd been in the park she'd felt like she belonged, like an islander who could relish the difference between herself and the off-islanders. On the other side of the wall, she was odd. People with whole shoes and complete shirts walked way around her in her raggedy shorts held up with a matted sweater tied around her waist. It hurt to be avoided. Fuck it. She was with her daughter, and if people avoided her, that was fine.

"Daddy married again so I could have a mother."

No comment.

Ted and Paloma kissed at the corner before the apartment building.

"He seems pretty cool," Roberta said. In his low-key way he protected Paloma without taking over.

"Yeah. He's cool." Then Roberta walked into the life that had gone on without her.

Roberta noticed the white gloves on the brass door handle. The kind of building that used to intimidate her. With a quiet nod, the doorman respectfully ignored Robbie's ensemble. Paloma smiled at his greeting, introduced Roberta, and gave not a glance to the spread of flowers giving glory in the five-gallon crystal vase on a claw-footed table in the center of the lobby. A checkerboard of black and white marble tiles spread across a quarter block of New York City real estate to two polished elevator doors. Fifth Avenue. John must have married well.

"Do you want to take the stairs?" Paloma asked. "We live on the twelfth floor." Why? Robbie wondered. Do I smell too bad to ride on the elevator? Is she afraid we'll run into someone who'll be distressed by a Black woman in rags? I hope she doesn't care about stuff like that. I did. And it made me unhappy. "Daddy told me you always took the stairs. He said you were very athletic."

The bronze elevator doors opened. Paloma slipped her hand inside Roberta's. It still felt small, as fragile as when she wasn't allowed to cross the street alone. Robbie would hold out her hand and Paloma would grab it and hold on until they reached the safety of the Shore of Sidewalk.

The elevator opened onto a small hallway with access to two apartments. Paloma opened the door on the left.

"Cynthia?" She yelled. Roberta followed through two large rooms.

Cynthia. A thin, muscular woman of a type not unlike Robbie met them in a hallway wiping her hands on a paper towel. White. At the end of the hall, beyond Cynthia, Roberta's image looked at Roberta from a mirror. Wild hair, varicolored skin, ragged bits and pieces of cloth and bark and grasses clinging and matted in hair and creases. She looked as if she'd been rolling around in dirt and mud, had been for years. Somehow, she'd thought she'd looked exotic, like one of the Brazilian tribesmen who hadn't been engulfed by modernity. The difference between what she thought and what was so made her laugh.

"Paloma, who is this?"

"Cynthia, meet Roberta Rose Williams, my mother. This is Cynthia Robbins, my stepmother." The bell rang.

"Excuse me, please," Cynthia said with only a slight catch in her throat.

"Is everything all right Miss Robbins?" A man's voice from the entry hall.

"Yes, we're all fine. Thanks for checking." And then louder, "We're fine, right Paloma?" Paloma stuck her head out of the sitting room. Robbie followed, her hands in the air. Look, nothing up my sleeves.

"We're fine, Mom. Hello, Mr. Simmons." Mr. Simmons pulled his bulk from the doorway.

"Paloma, can we talk privately for a moment? Please excuse us, Ms. Williams." Paloma had a lot of heart. Her stepmother, too. She seemed nice, considering. What must she be going through? Roberta had never had a derelict in her home; there was no real place at which she could relate to Cynthia's position. Beyond the entry hall was a small room, a closet, really, outfitted with an altar, with candles and dolls, a glass of clear liquid and a cigar. Santeria. Robbie understood then that Cynthia accepted the existence of spirits, that lives did not disappear totally, but disappeared only from the livings. Had Cynthia prayed that Paloma's mother's spirit might visit Paloma? If so, Cynthia was a gifted and powerful maker of prayers.

Robbie could see the park from Cynthia's windows. A mass of green. Trees. Grass. A shimmering brightness of water. She stared around the sitting room, and through the entry hall to the front door. Cynthia's home was tight with beautiful things. Toasters from the 1940's lined the kitchen pantry. Gleaming chrome, full of modern hope and optimism. Would Robbie have achieved a life as privileged as this for Paloma? Views of the park? Big rooms? Discreet, involved doormen?

Cynthia was back, her body between Roberta and Paloma.

"Can I get you something to drink? Water? Tea? Something stronger?"

"No, thank you." Robbie didn't know if she could eat or drink. She wasn't hungry or thirsty.

Cynthia was curious, but polite about it. "I guess a lot has changed." She tried to make conversation. Robbie didn't have much to say. She didn't think she was a living. More a wraith absent with leave. This was all new to her, too. She was just feeling her way.

Paloma said, "Mom, I think she'd like to get a shower."

What Robbie wanted was to stare at her daughter. To hear what happened when she was two and three and twelve and eight and nine and eleven and ten and thirteen. Did she have friends? Was she happy? Was it strange to have your mother again you after so many years? This was a dream, no? She was living her dream. To talk to her daughter as if her daughter had gone out to school one morning one age, and come back that afternoon years older. But first, make Cynthia more comfortable.

"Do you think I could have a bath?" Robbie said. Better than a shower for getting into nooks and creases. "If you leave me some cleanser and a sponge, I'll clean out the tub after myself."

"Don't be silly." Cynthia and Paloma took Roberta to a plain white bathroom with a basket of soaps on the floor and a cactus in the corner and gave her a fresh robe, a lined silk kimono, too nice to wear, really.

"It's the guest bathroom," Paloma said. "You don't have to worry about taking too long. Nobody else is using it." Just the kind of thing Robbie used to worry about. Inconveniencing people. Maybe she did still. Look how thoughtful her girl was.

Robbie took a shower, then a bath, then a shower. The water was heavy and warm, and if she closed her eyes she could forget how close the walls were and concentrate on the constant warmth. The water in the shower sped down the drain away from her, first black, then brown, then gray, then clear. By the time she came out of the bathroom, her husband was knocking around the kitchen getting himself a drink. He stood in the butler's pantry, a stranger's distance from her and asked if she wanted one.

"V and T? I bought some Dubonnet for you. You want that?" Those had been her staples, vodka and tonic, red Dubonnet on the rocks with lemon. What would it be like to have either one again?

"Thank you, no. Maybe later." Because the kimono was too fine to wear, Robbie stood naked in the hallway. It took a moment or two for her to remember that she should put some clothes on. Her mother would die, she who was always telling Robbie to "Put some lipstick on." She thought of the Duchess and realized that the old dame had long been unaware of how her nipples stared at people. Robbie was so much more like the Duchess than she was like the people in the apartment.

John looked good, his hair further back in the front where white was showing. He was still broad shouldered and flat stomached. Robbie tried to imagine the conversation that brought him home from wherever he'd been. Maybe:

"Honey, your dead wife is here. Could you come home?"

"I'll be right there." And then, "Excuse me, Mr. Bossman, my dead wife just dropped by, and I've got to go see her." Did his boss wonder why the ghost didn't just fly over to work instead? Isn't that how it worked?

Couldn't she just materialize in the office so his worker could keep on the job?

Or was the conversation:

"Paloma brought home a homeless woman who stinks, and Paloma's insisting it's her mother, and the homeless woman is saying it's so . . . I never saw her before, only her picture, I don't know if she looks like Paloma . . . I'm going to offer her a bar of soap and a towel and after that, I'm at the end of my rope. Right now, I'm going out to the elevator man and get him to keep checking on us here, but you'd better get home. I don't want to call the police, Paloma seems attached to the woman, and I could really use you here, she's your daughter and this woman says she's your wife, and I'm scared to put her out of the house because if she leaves, Paloma just might leave with her. How fast can you get here? . . . No, she's not violent, not yet, but I don't know what she'll do. To tell you the truth, I always found it really irresponsible that Roberta would go out running in Central Park in the middle of the night. You don't do that kind of thing when you have a child. That's crazy. So you cancel your meeting and get here right away."

John's wife offered Roberta a pair of raw silk pants. "I haven't worn them in fifteen pounds. You take them." They were lovely, sparkly and shiny with beads. Hostess pants. Robbie loved them. A lime green sleeveless shell, too, which Robbie wore to the dinner Paloma insisted they all have together.

"Of course we're having dinner, Cynthia. If you don't want to come it'll just be me and Dad." Roberta heard her from the hallway. Do all fifteen year old girls rule their mothers like this? Or is it peculiar to Paloma?

John's wife had Mozart playing as they sat around the dining table. The Requiem. Nothing wrong with her taste or her sense of humor. Outside, the day was lingering. Warm light colored the dining room gold. It was a sparkly room, mirrors and crystal and silver over shining dark wood. John sat at one end of the table, his wife at the other, Robbie across from Paloma who'd grown more gorgeous and fascinating in the last forty minutes.

"Everything looks so beautiful," Robbie said. Like an invited guest. For what do you do in a foreign situation but fall back on the familiar forms you learned at the very beginning? Please. Thank you very much. Could you pass the salt and pepper?

"So you were in the park all this time?" John's wife pushed her lettuce around with her fork.

"Yes." In her new clothes Robbie matched the room, her skin the same brown as the heart of pine floor, the beads on her new sleeveless shell glittering like the facets of the crystal in the china cabinet when she moved, the raw silk toreador pants nearly the same green as the seat cushions. Her hair was abundant, still wild, but clean. She looked the way she'd wanted to look when she was alive. She stopped gazing at her own reflection in the Moroccan mirror above the buffet, but not at her child across the table. Biology made Paloma a reflection, too; younger, her cheeks plumper and higher, her eyes brighter, her skin paler and more luminous. Robbie thought about how she'd refused to think about Paloma. And now. Now everyone was looking at her waiting for an answer.

"After a while outside the park becomes wallpaper, or backstage, behind the flats, not part of the play you're involved with at all. Plus, what was outside the park was brought in every morning. We'd eavesdrop on the conversations living people had, especially the runners and the ones who walked to and from work every day. We'd catch them on the way and on the way back."

"You said 'we'." John's wife seemed fascinated. But perhaps she was just a very good hostess.

"Yeah."

"So it wasn't lonely?" Dinner was make your own sandwiches. Sliced peasant bread. Sliced roast beef. Sliced tomatoes. Pickles. Garden greens. Brie to smear. Muscadet. Robbie put food on her plate and accepted wine in her glass. She couldn't eat it. Lonely? She was lonely now, at dinner with the people she knew best in the world. The same lonely as always. Where was the joy in each other's company passing between them like a yo-yo up and down a string? Would she ever race to these people and greet with hugs and kisses? Could that, perhaps, maybe, be the way she felt about everyone she knew? Close and connected. Other people had that, and she could, too. That would be Heaven.

"It must have been frustrating to be so close, and unable to connect."

"You're very perceptive." That was honest.

"You tried, though, right, Mommy?"

Mommy.

It split the air like lightning, the memory of it floated down like fireworks. Robbie's first "Mommy", not counting the mami's our brothers of Hispanic descent would shout from their stoops when Robbie walked by. The most Paloma had managed before Robbie died was a "ma" sound. Robbie could see John's face in Paloma, and John in the length of Paloma's limbs, the narrowness of her hips, the curve of her bottom lip. But "Mommy" signaled Paloma's recognition of her connection to Robbie, and that's what made it so. Robbie felt sorry for John's wife. How must it be for her, to have a woman come from the dead sitting at her table, claiming the child who lived in her home, carrying the love her husband's heart poured when he was young?

"John is very lucky to have you." Robbie said.

"We're both lucky," Cynthia said. "Very lucky." She reached across the table and covered his hand with hers. Bitch.

No. No. "Your home is so beautiful." And it was. Not intimidating, homey. Some things old, some new, some very worn and much-loved. So they conversed.

John no longer acted; he was involved in fundraising for disadvantaged city youth. He wrote reports and took people, many of them his wife's friends, to lunch during which he'd charm them out of money for his organization. He called it "picking their pockets". He was good at it and moderately well paid. Paloma was considering going to a high school for fine artists, or maybe one for performing artists. Robbie suggested Paloma go to both, do high school twice. Why not? What better way to identify what you really liked than practicing it a few times a day every weekday? And then contrasting it with the learning and practicing of something else? Robbie felt she was talking too much. Not making sense. She used to have such a fine mind. But her heart had fed on it. She was thinking crazy.

Robbie wanted to touch Paloma, to stick her face in Paloma's hair, feel the space in the hollow of her throat, wrap her hand span around Paloma's waist. She wanted to feel the physical-ness of her daughter so strong and graceful, like a woodsy plant. Here she was, not a collection of old memories, but a living, spontaneous being with thoughts and gestures and habits that Robbie had never imagined. The girl had favorite colors, and shoes, and songs she danced to. Paloma wasn't a baby any more, and her body was her own and even her mother, even her mother, had to let her body be her own. But Roberta wanted to touch her. God, she wanted to. And wasn't that her failure in life, that she hadn't done the things she wanted? She squeezed the leg of the chair she sat in.

Robbie couldn't eat this food. She chewed on something. Swallowed. The room was oppressively hot. In the park, if she were hot she could climb to the top of a tree and catch a breeze, or crawl into a shadow. In the park, she could move. She couldn't do that here.

It was true. Robbie shouldn't have gone out that night, not when she had a baby at home. If she'd stayed home, gone to bed, she would have seen her girl grow up; she would have had an influence, her presence would be part of how her daughter interpreted the world. She would have grown herself, too. Perhaps to have an apartment as nice as this one, or one even better, with a view of the river.

And this was a surprise: she still loved John. His face pulled her hormones to high tide like the full moon the sea, her emotions listing in the waves. He made her shy about a body she'd forgotten about, and proud of it, too. See? My stomach is flat again. Concave, actually. I fit into pants that are too small for your wife, and she's skinny. White skinny. How silly to have never outgrown the body concerns of high school.

"I don't think any of us is very hungry." John's wife said. "Why don't I just put this stuff in the refrigerator and if anybody's hungry later, we'll help ourselves? Paloma, help me, please."

Robbie stood to help. John's wife took her plate.

"Paloma and I can handle this. I may take her to my mother's after we stack the dishwasher."

"I was hoping we could spend more time together."

"It's been such an emotionally strenuous day. I think she'll sleep better at my mother's."

"I don't." Paloma said.

"We'll discuss it later."

Robbie allowed John to lead her by her elbow down a hallway lined with cabinets and backlit treasures. John's hair was lighter, the color mixed with white and gray now, highlighting his temples. When they first shared a pillow she'd stare at his hair, its many colors, red and blond and platinum. What things had she been angry with him about? She couldn't remember. This was the love of her youth. When she had been all preparation and possibility, he had been her choice, this beautiful man with a lovely voice and fingers as thin as her own. She had loved his love of fun. The only reason or planning he ever needed was "I want to." She'd loved that once, so different from her and her lists and budgets.

John turned into to a small room with a noisy air conditioner. The pull-out couch from their old living room was there, a brown leather two-seater. John wavered between the desk and the couch.

"I didn't live, for a year. I cried and got mad at myself for crying. I kicked myself in the ass for not moving on one day, and the next tried to honor the process of grieving. I got scared that I would drift forever, never seeing beyond the next task, get Paloma to preschool, pick Paloma up, fix dinner. Your mother came every week and did the laundry. That was nice. She ironed Paloma's tiny clothes, and my shirts. She ironed creases into my jeans. She ironed the sheets. She was good company. She fixed dinner those days, too, and fried apples for Paloma when she got home. In the evenings Roy picked her up. Since they were in the city already, they would go to Teachers for dinner. They'd always invite us. Paloma liked restaurants, even then. So Claire would pack up what she cooked and she and Roy would take us out for dinner, then we'd eat what Claire cooked the next day. Your mother died six years ago."

He offered a photograph from his desk. John and Paloma with Claire and Roy on the deck outside the older couple's country house.

"You father died a little over a year later. Squamous carcinoma, very rare, usually seen in areas of the Far East where people chew beetle nuts. His heart was broken. He tried to patch it up. Then he stopped. I think I pulled it together because I couldn't tell myself any more that Paloma would have them if anything happened to me.

"This is so strange, and I'm so glad it's happening. For me, for Paloma."

Robbie walked into his chest, laid her head on his heart and listened to it beating. He enfolded her in his arms.

Should she have felt guilty? He was married to someone else, someone decent and sensitive. She felt love. He was her husband, too, and the father of her child, and she had married him first. "I am so sorry. So sorry. I always loved you. I always loved you. Even when I was angry at you, up to here with your temper, even when I threatened to leave, I loved you. I never wanted anyone but you.

"When I was in the park, whenever I thought of you, I felt hollow, so I made myself stop. Paloma, too. I made myself not think of you, and that's how I survived. I closed off parts of my heart, the parts I loved best. I just shut that door and painted over it, like it wasn't there," Robbie said. John rubbed her head, a slight pressure from his fingertips onto her scalp. He remembered. She spoke into his armpit.

"I had a friend when I was in the Park named Ivan, a funny, friendly man. We used to entertain each other with happy memories from our lives. I told him about trips we took, about Greece, and the plane coming back for us at LaGuardia, but I never mentioned you. I never told him about the loveliness of a fresh warm infant falling asleep on my chest, or how a one-year-old's sweet arms felt wrapped around my neck. I didn't tell him about you and me being in love and how that made all of it cool. Not thinking of it isn't the same as forgetting."

She remembered how sweet it was to breathe in John's smell, to be protected in his white boy entitlement, a gift he bore without knowing that he had it.

John talked into the top of her head. "You don't know what it was like to miss you. The first Christmas, I slept in front of the television. I never went to the bedroom, except to get my clothes. I woke up with snot dried on my face. For months."

This was her heart, her husband, the man who pulled her inside his robe against his naked body before she went to work. Why had that made her angry instead of glad? How had she ignored how much he loved her? How much she loved him?

"Do you know what it was to live without you? With Paloma growing into your face, holding her head the way you held your head?" He stopped and breathed. "I should have stopped you from going out."

"You were asleep. I was careful not to wake you."

"I should have waited up. I should have gone with you. We could have gotten a sitter. It was a big deal; you were up for an award."

“I was okay with it. With you not coming. It was expensive.”

“Still...” John smelled like John. A good smell, like fun in summer and rum in winter, and apples and grass, and pot. “I was awake when you came home.”

John cried. His body shook; grief, fresh as the moment the phone call came, swayed him. He doubled up, crushing Robbie inside his silent sobs. “I could have stopped you. I let you go.”

And what could she say? It was true. If he had challenged her, she might not have gone.

“I wanted to go, and I didn’t want to argue about it. I was glad you were asleep.” She couldn’t tell if he heard her. She pulled herself away. “It’s not your fault, John. I did what I wanted. I would forgive you, but there’s nothing to forgive. I don’t hold it against you. If it had turned out differently, I’d even have thanked you. It was a beautiful night. I had a great run. A really great run.

“I love you. I always loved you. Even when I was mad at you, I loved you. When you were riding my last nerve and I was telling you about it, I was in love with your ass. I worried all the time that you didn’t know. That I didn’t tell you. I’m telling you now. I loved being with you, I loved me with you.” Robbie laughed. “Death means never getting to say I’m sorry.”

John had a boner. If Robbie’d been a man, she’d have had one, too. She didn’t care about his wife who had been kind to her and given her dinner and a bath, and clothes. It wasn’t her fault that she’d married a dead woman’s husband and the dead woman came back. She was a nice woman, but nice doesn’t protect anyone from anything. Robbie’d spent her whole life being nice.

They made love in the way they'd made love in the loft bed in their first tiny bedroom, urgent, with humor, with Robbie's hand over John's mouth because he was noisy when he came.

Night

Paloma, who came back home with tears on her face and a bag of ice cream, and John's wife took Robbie to the guest room, which was also the room from which John's wife sold antique musical instruments. Every surface was covered with a labeled instrument from another century. From the wall hung Guitar, Spanish, sixteenth century. Mandolin, French, Belle Epoch. On the window seat: Child's harp, fourteenth century. And another just like it on a bureau. The bed was antique and narrow, with a headboard and footboard painted with pink roses and moss green garlands on cream. It was a bed both French provincial and girly girl. "Was this your bed?" Robbie asked Paloma.

"Yes."

The sheets smelled good. The blanket folded on the foot of the bed still had its tag. Saks Fifth Avenue. Robbie lay in the bed. She watched the sheet rise and fall on her chest. Every once in a while the curtain at the window fluttered. There was dust on the windowsill. Light from the moon bounced on the leaves in Central Park. Was it time enough for all to be asleep? Or was everyone else up, secreted in a bedroom watching television with the sound down low, so as not to disturb her? Or to keep the television watching secret from her?

Robbie dreamed she was floating in a Nordic sky over a Caribbean Sea. Green swathes of light surrounded her and the air was music, a murmuring of voices and string and wind instruments and rhythm like hearts beating. She was floating and it was cool and warm and free. She looked at her hands and arms and legs and they were all glowing, shining like stars. It was a happy, gentle dream, sailing with no thought of danger, only iridescent, breezy peace. When she had been alive and Paloma was a baby she'd made up little visions to tell the child as she fell asleep. Sailing in the sky among the stars was one of them. A tiny view of a little piece of Robbie's Heaven.

Robbie woke refreshed. What time was it? She folded back the bedclothes to let the bed air out. She walked quietly in the hush of the apartment, not so dark, lit from outside lights, past the hallway bathroom and the dining room to Paloma's bedroom. It was messy, shoes on the floor, clothes at the bottom of the bed, a damp towel ruining the wood of her footboard. Robbie sat on the edge of her daughter's bed and watched her breathe. Wasn't it strange that she should be so easily accommodated back into life? Here she was in her husband's and daughter's new home, with their new wife and mother, in fine clothing, after a good hot shower, with clean skin and clean hair. Was she accommodated so seamlessly because she was temporary? People can put up with anything if they know it's just momentary. If she were a living, she wouldn't go on living at Paloma's house. She'd get a job, rent a place and finish a book to sell – if she could read and write. On Paloma's desk was a paper. Robbie picked it up to see if she could read it. She couldn't. No matter. She could tell a story, still. Hah! What a story she had to tell. And what was the moral to the story? What was the point? What did she have to share with the world to make life more full? What wisdom, what advice, what words of infinite guidance? Don't worry, be happy? Be true to yourself? Betray no one? If it feels bad, don't do it? Love freely? Is that all she had? A haphazard list of slogans?

John's wife came to the door, silent as a wraith.

"How is it for you to raise a Black child?" Robbie whispered.

"Well, she's not very black, is she? She's more the color of. . ."

"Of a peach."

"Yes. Just what I was going to say. When she's sleeping, her cheek looks like you could bite into it. People who know me know she's not my biological. And the ones who don't . . . amuse me."

Did this woman, this woman who wasn't the child's mother, did she watch the child while she slept, bend her cheek to the child's nose to check that the child was breathing? Did she snuggle her ear on the child's neck and smell the child's sweet dreams? Robbie felt those smells belonged to her, that no one had a right to sniff the still-a-baby smell just beneath Paloma's ears but her. Did John's wife spoon up with Paloma when the child was afraid in the dark? Robbie remembered a succession of little nightlights. A blue angel that they'd lost almost immediately. A plain one they'd put colored Christmas bulbs in. One with a Dalmatian that fell off.

"Yes." Cynthia said. The two women were still in the silence. The living one nibbling at the edge of her glass of sherry, the dead one relishing the near dark. In the park, noise was constant. The murmur of traffic ever there, like waves at the end of the ocean, always coming, always pulling away. The crunch of footsteps, some hard, some slow, voices. Not always, but often enough, there was the wind in the leaves, wind on its own. Not here. Windows and drapes, bricks and mortar kept it out. The clock on the wall was a metronome of time passing, never losing a tick or a tock on and on and on.

"I wonder what she'll make of all this," Cynthia said. "I wonder what I'll make of it."

And then later, "She's a wonderful girl. She'll make a great life for herself." Robbie was grateful to this woman for loving her child, but she did not want to share with her. When Robbie next noticed, Cynthia was gone.

Robbie crept under the covers with her sleeping daughter, put her knees behind Paloma's knees, her hips behind Paloma's hips, and her shoulders behind Paloma's shoulders. No matter that Paloma was longer than she, Robbie wrapped Paloma inside and enjoyed Paloma's smell, a warm meld of soap and lotion and Paloma skin. Paloma snuggled into Robbie's deep breathing and Robbie fell into dreamless sleep.

A clock chimed twelve when Robbie let herself out of the apartment. She hoped no one would be upset that she hadn't locked the door behind her; she didn't have a key.

A different doorman tipped his hat at Robbie as he held the door open and she stepped out into the night. The city was wide-awake. Trains rumbled under the street. People ran for taxis and spilled out of busses. There was laughter, and grumbling and fast motion all over. Light glowed everywhere. From street lamps and apartment windows and tops of taxis and billboards and awnings and headlights from cars whizzing by in the dark that wasn't dark.

Skirting the park, she walked down to Fifty-Ninth, west to Broadway, up to Eighty-sixth, and over to Riverside. She waited for an M5 bus. "Your fare," the bus driver said, but he didn't make her get off when she didn't pay. She looked at Riverside Park. It was a nicer park than Central Park, really, with the river's presence beyond. She had never taken the M5 ride for granted; alive she'd known it was lovely, the grand mansions and apartment buildings on one side, the park and river and the Palisades on the other, and she enjoyed it now. She waved goodbye when the bus turned onto 72nd Street. She looked forward to crowds. That's what she wanted now. Mingling among live people. At Lincoln Center she got off. The music store she expected to find was gone. She found a dance club in the fifties near the West Side Highway. The bouncers at the door waved her in.

It was dark, and loud, and sweaty. The pulse of the party came through the floor and through the air. If she came back, she would open a place like this. Would she like that? She was sure it had an ugly side as well as the glamour side. Robbie stepped high, held her arms up and twirled her hands on her wrists. Very glad that someone else had taken the trouble and made this place. She staggered onto the street.

She wanted to smell the bakeries and walked down, traveling east, then west, east and west again. Some guys cruised her, she ignored them, they moved on. She ended up near the tunnel to Jersey where the air was thick and sweet with butter and sugar. Robbie sat on a loading platform and smelled it. One of the workers came out to have a cigarette. "Nice night," he said. "Yes, indeed," she said. And it was: the sky was clear, the moon was bright and silver, the air was warm. A very good night.

When Paloma was new, it'd been strange to walk the streets with the baby. To appear as a family outside the hospital felt so exposed, so insecure. Robbie had started this evening with that feeling, startled and amazed and overwhelmed. By now, New York embraced her. New York was an aunt who'd let you drink wine and didn't tell your parents. New York was a woman who liked you. New York was easy. She wouldn't hurt you, but she'd break your heart.

Robbie was heading back uptown, through Washington Square Park, Herald Square, Bryant Park, Grand Central Station, so stunningly lit and beautiful, Paley Park with its waterfall. (She wasn't sure, but she thought perhaps there was a wraith there. She saw some signs, probably nothing. Still, might they mean that wraiths were afterliving all over the city?) Robbie made her way uptown sticking to the East Side after 59th Street. She didn't want to set foot in Central Park. Call it superstition.

Morning

The sky was lightening. Maintenance men hosed off the sidewalks. As she passed, they held their hoses away from her, politely. She wanted to feel the water. When she'd been a child in Queens, playing in the backyard on hot afternoons, her parents watered her and her brother and sister like hardy plants. The kids would run and scream on the crew-cut lawn, set neatly between two stucco garages, bordered thickly on three sides with flowers of Tahitian intensity.

At dawn Robbie sat on a park bench across the street from Paloma's building so close to the park Robbie suspected it could suck her back inside if it wanted. Were there wraiths behind her on the other side of the park wall? She refused to turn around and see. Because what if she couldn't see?

She saw John come out of his building. He looked harried. And why not? His family's life had been tossed into disarray. Robbie imagined he was figuring out would he and his new wife put her up? Would she move into the guest bedroom with all the antiques? Would she be demanding of his sexual attentions? And in the midst of all of this *what is happening?* she'd deserted him again. Were they hoping she was gone for good? Worried about her whereabouts? Did they, in the light of a new day, even believe her? Robbie had dropped a bomb on

John. She knew it. In life she'd dropped bombs on him, too. "If you don't do something around here, I'm leaving you." "If you don't clean out the car, I'm getting rid of it."

Robbie settled on her space on the bench. Sometime, Paloma would come out. And what would Robbie tell her? Should she tell her daughter that nothing matters but the doing? That plans are nothing. Tomorrow is nothing. To use her mind, use her body, enjoy her senses? To challenge anyone, anything that would keep her still? No, not to challenge, but not to submit. To close her life to the influence of anyone who does not want the best for her. To be, now.

Robbie had lived for later. Saving money for when she retired. Saving the clothes that she loved best for special occasions that never came. Her good suits for meetings that somehow were never the meetings she had. There was a rich life in her closet, incredible meals that stayed in her cabinets, books that were too frivolous to write that stayed in her head because she didn't see how she'd get paid for doing them. Please, Paloma. Do what pleases you. Be an artist. Answer only "What do I want?" That is the hardest question, and the only one that will lead you to your happiness.

Is that what she should say to Paloma? To always be active. What about the sweetness and the knowledge that came from being still? Life goes on within you and without you?

"I saw you from my room," Paloma said. She sat down next to her mother. The two had the same high cheekbones and broad forehead, the same shape eyes. Their coloring was all different. Paloma was golden and orange and green, while Robbie was brown from top to bottom. They were like two birds of the same species, one spectacular male, one modest female. "Why did you leave?"

"I was out of place."

"I think you should get an apartment near ours, I mean mine and Daddy's and Cynthia's. In the same building. Then we could be like a family, but you'd still have your privacy. I'm sure you could publish about being dead. It's such a strange story. It'd be a great movie. How you come back and everything's changed."

What would happen if she stayed, Robbie wondered. She would write a book. It might become a little known esoteric work gathering dust in a bookstore's metaphysical section, or it could be huge. Robbie was sure she could make it huge. Would her sales go through the roof? Yes. She could take Paloma around the world. They could learn languages together. She'd be a mother to be proud of. One who traveled. Who was on Oprah. Was Oprah still on TV? Robbie bet she was.

"We could go shopping, or to the movies or something. Have coffee," Robbie said.

"I'd like to go with you." Paloma said.

"What things do you want to do? Do you want to go to Africa? Italy?"

"Daddy took me. He said you and he went. He took me to Greece, too. There were lots of Germans there. I didn't like them very much. I liked the ocean. I could float in it without trying."

"I liked Greece."

"Daddy showed me pictures. You looked happy." They occupied the bench together. "You're leaving?"

"Yes, I'm leaving. Before you go to Heaven, you get messages through your dreams. Heaven dreams, they're called and they're different for everybody. Last night I had my first one. Today I've been wondering if it would have been better for me to see you and not make myself known to you. I'm making you lose your mother twice and giving you an experience that if you tell people about it, they'll look at you strange. All so I could have more experience of you."

Paloma banged her back against the bench.

Again and again like a mantra. As if she could pay for change with pain.

"I'm glad you came. I wanted to know what you were like, too. Daddy would tell me things, but it wasn't the same. You were like a princess in a story, or Georgia Nicolson, someone like that." Paloma sat in her space on the bench and tears spilled out of her face. She gritted her teeth tight and bit the inside of her cheeks; Robbie could see it.

"Your life sucked, didn't it?" Paloma said.

"Whatever do you mean?" That's how Robbie used to talk when she wanted to pretend she didn't understand the questions. English from England, via Hollywood, or the BBC. Robbie laughed. She was actually becoming quite funny to herself. She sighed. "No. My life didn't suck. You're my daughter. With that alone…

"I had talent and a husband who loved me and was intelligent, I had work that at times I enjoyed. Good things. I had a very nice life.

"I had a friend in the afterlife. We were both writers, and before she went to Heaven, we'd tell each other stories based on our memories. You want to do that? I'll tell you something I loved about my life and then, you tell me a time when you were loving your life. I'll start. Okay?

"I remember standing in my kitchen and looking out over the Hudson. I had just prepared oatmeal for you, dished it into a deep white bowl with fluted sides.

We'd bought the bowl from the remainders and incomplete sets and broken stuff room at Ikea. It was a simple and honest bowl, with integrity, but humble. I scooped out a hole in the center of the oatmeal for margarine. I swirled a knife through the surface of the cereal and poured maple syrup in the swirl. I poured some orange juice into a plastic cup for you and pushed on the cap. It had a spout in it to drink from. A sippy cup. Out the window a proud-breasted cement barge powered down the river. I was happy. I remember in that moment being very happy, and aware of it.

"Do you have a happy memory for me?"

"The best part in the 6th grade play was Rosie Alvarez. It had the most lines and the most solos. I tried out for it." Paloma beamed. In that moment Robbie saw she was a child in the process of becoming and Robbie was both proud and afraid. "In the first audition I sang, 'What did I ever see in him?' and 'An English Teacher,' and I had to act the opening scene. Then I got called back for a second audition, and this time they had me and two other girls try out for Kim, she's the girl Conrad Birdie is going to kiss on TV before he's inducted into the army. And after I auditioned, the Musical Director took my face in her hands and said, 'You're so talented.' They were supposed to announce the casting in December before the holiday break, but they didn't. Daddy complained to them in January. And one afternoon in February, Mr. Derman, the drama teacher and the Director called the sixth grade into the auditorium and said, '20% of you are going to be happy, and 80% of you will be disappointed.' Then they called the roles and the names of the kids who got the parts from the smallest parts to the biggest. Teenagers. Little Brother. The Mayor. Mrs. McAfee. Kim McAfee. The Mayor's wife. Albert's mother. Conrad Birdie. Albert.

They called almost all the parts and not my name. I thought I'd get something, and I hadn't gotten anything. I thought, 'Since I know tap, maybe I'll be the choreographer.' Two parts remained. Albert and Rose. David Holmes. Paloma Roberts."

They sat together for a long time. Robbie told Paloma about the Fauves and Ivan, and the Duchess, and what it was like to afterlife outside? She told her about learning to fight and being comfortable with violence. About using the livings for entertainment. What else could Robbie give? Answers? She didn't have any.

Do I need to live until she's old enough to be told the foolish things I wanted and the terrible things I did to get them.

Paloma told about winning a bet with her science teacher. Robbie told about her first meeting with a friend who would become life-long in college, about sunbathing in Jamaica, about the peasants and their daughter who married a king's son. The sun warmed their faces and blazed inside their clothing.

Robbie said, "Know what Heaven is?

"Everyone in Heaven is pure thought and feeling and experience, instantly available and availing of all we all are. Heaven is an ocean of thought. Sometimes we fly off of a wave and out of the ocean and evaporate to the sky and join clouds and float over the earth, and then fall to earth to feed plants or rinse a dirty old man's butt. When we return to that ocean of thought, we are richer in experience than we had been, with more to share in the constant loving and sharing that's Heaven.

"Be whatever you want. Be many things. One at a time or all at once. Just because you're a writer doesn't mean you can't be a carpenter, or an actor or a dress designer or a secretary. You don't have to be the top of your field. That's not a good goal. It's a dumb goal. It's not even a goal. It's a by-product. Like dust in a woodshop. Like the kitchen warming up when you bake a cake. It's a by-product of loving what you do. I never loved writing the way I should have. I never loved your Dad, a wonderful person, brave and scared, and scarred and warm, the way I might have. In all my life, I was unconditional only with you.

"Be unconditional with everyone. With everything. Am I scaring you?"

"No, Mommy."

Mommy. Robbie could not twist her face any way that would keep her from crying.

She could stay. She could get an advance, she could dictate the book, she could raise her daughter. That was sure. Whether she was John's wife or not she was Paloma's mother. How lovely she was. Independent, articulate, proud and kind. Look how her daughter had turned out. Could Robbie herself have done a better job? What would she hobble her daughter with? What self-defeating fears would she pass on?

"Life was like God was courting me. A perfect suitor. Someone my parents liked. Respectful, serious, but not stiff, ambitious and kind. Someone who had influence and often wielded it on my behalf. Someone who gave great, extravagant gifts. But because there were gifts from God, I didn't care about them. I put them on the side and longed over what God didn't give me. Even if it was not as good as what I already had. If God gave me a designer fur coat, I couldn't be happy unless I got a dungaree vest."

Paloma smiled. Robbie kissed her. She kissed Robbie.

"More things than I can imagine are possible," Robbie said.

Exo and his boys were spread across the entranceway to the Conservatory Gardens when Robbie came back. The boys who used to scare her, long, long ago. She'd tucked them in.

Exo wanted to know, everyone wanted to know, "How was it?" She felt like Marco Polo back from a land they had never seen and could not dream.

"Wonderful. Excellent. My daughter is so cool. She's smart and funny and kind and inventive and silly and serious and so beautiful. Her legs go on forever. I can see my face in her face. That makes me happy.

"I fell in love with my husband again. He's grown up nice. Trying to be responsible. New York takes my breath away." She caught her breath. "It was a nice place to visit, but I don't want to live there.

"You seen Ivan? Know where he is?"

"Ivan?"

"Yeah." Why was Exo suddenly so peculiar?

"Ivan went to Heaven the moment you left the park. He got tired of waiting for you. He said he'll see you later."

"He went to Heaven? But what about the rules?"

"What about them?"

The End

Acknowledgements

If it takes a village, mine is a hamlet, small but mighty. I thank Lisbeth Mark, boss lady of Bow Bridge Communications, for her encouragement over many years. Lizzie Ross, author of *Kenning Magic*, for her careful reading and incisive comments. Leesa Kellam for boots-on-the ground advice while keeping my head to the sky. In the sister lottery, I hit the jackpot.

For keeping me on the path and pulling me over the finish line, I thank Joel Cohen. For their scholarship I thank the authors of *The Park and the People*, Roy Rosenzweig and Elizabeth Blackmar.

Finally, I thank my lucky stars for Deanna Drew whose belief and steady support in all things is dearer to me than I can say. I thank her for giving this book its title.

Cover design: Daren Koniuk

Made in the USA
Middletown, DE
25 September 2019